IT'S
THEIR
WAY

IT'S THEIR WAY

a novel

by

BRUCE K BECK

AUDACITY BOOKS

WE DARE TO TELL THE TRUTH

New York

This is a first edition from Audacity Books.
Please visit us on the web at www.audacitybooks.com.
For information about rights or purchases,
please email us at info@audacitybooks.com.

This book is dedicated to all the soldiers in the front lines of food service.

Chapter One

The day I met Cole, I thought my heart was impervious. I thought I would never be able to accept anything from another man. And I thought I had nothing to give. Yet, when we shook hands and Cole sat down across from the desk in my little office, I began to wonder if perhaps I wanted to live again, after all.

The previous year had been steeped in pain. When Jamie left me, I didn't have all that much interest in living. I thought we had had two perfect years together. Or perhaps I thought we had had two *slightly* imperfect years together that would lead to something even better. Whatever I was really thinking, I assumed we were all in. I thought we'd keep living and loving—together—until we ended up in a retirement home—together. But one day Jamie told me he was leaving.

"Why?" I begged to know. He couldn't tell me, he said. He just needed to move on, he said. He did *not* say, "Can't we be friends?" Jamie's a smart man. He wouldn't pull shit like that knowing that I always have my knife roll with me. Did I consider taking out a long, narrow blade and plunging it into Jamie's faithless heart? No. I loved him too desperately to consider anything violent. I'd have sooner turned a blade on myself. But none of that is who I am.

"Justin Alexander," I said as I rose from my desk chair and extended my hand.

"Cole Watkins," he said as he shook my hand. "I think you have my resumé."

"Yes, Cole, I've read it," I said. "Please sit." We settled in and sized each other up. Cole had a lot to recommend him: a certificate from a reputable culinary school in DC; some work experience in name-brand restaurants in Chicago and New Orleans; letters from teachers and bosses that were filled with glowing praise. I suspected he would make a perfect replacement for my *sous-chef*—my assistant, really. Harvey was moving to Las Vegas soon with his wife and child. I wished him well, but I also felt his loss keenly. Could Cole maybe take his place?

Another quality about Cole, which I noted first thing, was that he was exceptionally beautiful: medium brown skin with a healthy sheen to it; a trim body that I suspected was quite strong; large, golden eyes; and a radiant smile. Cole exuded an appealing combination of strength and sweetness. I was smitten. I also knew he was the perfect candidate to fill my open position. I offered him the job.

"Thank you, Chef," he said. "I'd like to work under you, if the terms are okay." I filled Cole in on hours, pay, benefits, all the business stuff. It was a generous deal, more or less—if any job in the restaurant business could actually be considered good. We do it because we have a burning need to cook. Like actors, I suspect most of us would do something else if we had any other talent. Cole had the need. I could read it in his face. Yes, he was one of us. And now he would become part of my team. A very important part of my team, if all went well.

We sealed the deal with another handshake. I asked Cole if he could trail tonight's dinner shift, and tomorrow's as well, and then start on Thursday. He said he could. I offered to go over the menu with him the next afternoon, after he had had a taste of our kitchen culture. He agreed. Cole was bright and energized. I had no worries about getting him up to speed quickly. He went home to change.

Chef de Cuisine is an interesting position. I was responsible for every morsel of food that left the kitchen and every worker, right down to the dishwashers. But it was not my restaurant. It was not even my kitchen, really. And it was not my menu—except for daily specials, all of which had to be cleared with the Executive Chef. It was *his* kitchen and *his* menu. I served at his pleasure, not that he seemed to have much pleasure in him.

To be fair, Jeremy Talbot was too busy being an international celebrity to be much of a presence in the restaurant. It was *almost* my kitchen. I think, at the time, I was almost content to take all the responsibility for the finished product without taking the credit—or the blame—for the inspiration. It was my career at the time. I accepted it. I was maybe more concerned about my private life, or lack thereof.

That was my reality when Cole came to work for me. He settled into the job and the team quickly, as I knew he would. Saturday dinner was particularly hectic, as usual. Cole was unflappable. He completed his plates with precision and orderly grace. I was impressed, I must say. When the rush was over, I said to him, "How about a beer tonight, after the shift?"

"Sure," he said. I'd never been quite so relieved to finish a workday. When everything was spotless, I closed the kitchen for the night. Cole followed me out the kitchen door and into the street. I felt a gust of autumn wind on my face. It acted like a tonic. Some people don't think of New York City as being bathed in fresh air, but it is, of course. And whenever the weather is cool, the contrast between the kitchen and the outside world is striking. I breathed in deeply. We headed to a bar.

"I know I said beer, but I prefer wine, most of the time. They have a good Malbec here. I'm going to have that. What would you like?"

"I'll have the same," Cole said. I ordered.

"Thanks, Cole, for being a quick study. You did great tonight."

"Thank you, Justin, for trusting me," Cole said. "I like your team. But then I knew I would. It's a top-down thing. A quality leader inspires quality."

"That's sweet, Cole. Thanks for that," I said. "I know something about your history, but I'd like to know more about *you*. I like to know the man I'm going to be elbow-to-elbow with." Was I flirting? Maybe. Cole smiled. Warmly.

"Justin, I'll tell you anything. Well, *almost* anything. Some things are for when we know each other better, and some things are for after *many* glasses of wine."

"I can be a patient man, sometimes. I'll settle for the basics," I said. "And then I'll wait for the rest."

Cole smiled broadly, sipped his wine, and said, "When I was a kid, I was dying to get out of Georgia. I had some great schoolteachers back home. I loved them, and I loved my grandmother, but not much else. They and my church helped me get to culinary school. I almost went to Howard instead. But I wanted to cook so strongly that culinary won out. I liked it. It was a lot of hard work, and the after-school jobs were tough, too, but I did it.

"I also spent Sunday mornings at a museum or a library, and DC has plenty of both, of course. Those tough old ladies at school taught me there's a great big world out there. I wanted a bite of it. I tried to continue my education. I think I'm backsliding these days. The museum visits stopped when I had my first DC boyfriend. I'm gay, of course. I'm sure you knew that."

"I'm relieved," I said. "I have a really strong urge to kiss you, and I don't normally like kissing straight men."

"Interesting," Cole said. "I've been wanting to kiss you, too. What are we going to do about this?"

"I think we should go to my apartment and kiss. That's my best idea. What do you think?"

"I think that's brilliant," Cole said. "But first, I'd like to know a little bit about the man I'll be kissing."

"Fair enough," I said. "I grew up in a boring little town in northern Connecticut." I didn't share much more about my childhood. I wasn't ready to tell him the kinds of things he needed to know to understand me. That could wait, surely. "I had lots of college dreams, and I was accepted at Yale and Brown, but I couldn't quite commit to either of them. So I went to Johnson & Wales. I got some liberal arts. I don't regret a single philosophy class. But all I really wanted was culinary training. And I got it.

"You've met Scott. We were classmates. As soon as I started this job, I reached out and asked him to run lunch. He said yes. And he's been my anchor ever since. Scott's a morning person. He likes working during the day and then going home to his family. I adore him. I couldn't do my job without him. And I'm beginning to feel the same way about you, Cole. Could we maybe leave history there, for tonight?"

"Yes, Justin. I'll wait for the next installment. But I'm not very good at waiting for a kiss." I paid the bar tab, and we headed out. There were only about ten blocks between the bar and my apartment, but I wasn't willing to invest ten minutes in a walk when a cab could get us there in two. And it did. I said goodnight to Carlos, the night doorman, and we headed upstairs. The elevator seemed particularly slow. Or was it my eagerness to taste Cole?

I invited him in. We didn't get very far past the transom before we grabbed each other and shared our first kiss. It was deep and lovely. I paused long enough to bolt the door and drop our jackets on the chair, and then I led Cole to my bedroom. "It's so late, and it was such a long day. I'll bet I smell like a pig," I said.

"I like pigs," Cole said. "And I love the way you smell."

"In that case—my sty," I said, as I ushered him to my bed. "Let's wallow." We stripped quickly. No teasing. "Jesus, Cole, I'm in awe. You're even more gorgeous than I imagined."

"Thanks, Justin, but I came here for kisses—not speeches."

"Quite right," I said. I gave Cole a gentle push that landed him squarely in the middle of my bed. And then I took a dive that landed me right beside him. I reached for him. He reached for me. We got right to the business of kissing as deeply as we could manage. I lost track of whose tongue was whose. We blended. We held each other tenderly. We slipped into a melding embrace that felt primal to me, as if our bodies were meant to be joined. As if I had been searching for the half of me that was missing and had only just found it.

There would be other nights for exploration, I hoped. I was certain I would find a lot to like about Cole's body. But our first time together, neither of us was willing to lose our embrace long enough to experiment. Instead, we lay there in my bed, all tongues and arms, with our pelvises tightly joined as well. Two raging hard-ons were as one. My breathing quickened and became like a pant. Cole's mirrored mine.

Before much longer, we both erupted in joyous spasms. We continued to hold each other and to kiss deeply as we recovered. Only when our breathing had normalized and my body felt as limp as a dishrag did I release him. Tentatively. We started to laugh. Cum comes in various textures and colors, of course. In our case, the viscosity and the whiteness and the opalescence were identical. It appeared as if we had produced one huge load. We tasted it and kissed some more.

"Cole, I'm speechless," I said.

"Me, too," he said. We lay there for a while longer. Silent.

Eventually I broke through the quiet to say, "Please tell me you'll sleep over. I couldn't bear to stop holding you. Tomorrow morning maybe I'll be able to let go, but not tonight."

"Yes, Justin," Cole said. "I couldn't leave your bed right now if I wanted to. I'm not sure I can walk."

"Good," I said. "Let me know if I can get you a toothbrush, or anything. Otherwise, I intend to stay right here."

"Good," he said. "That's where I want you." We finally got up to pee and to brush our teeth, and then we headed right back to bed. As I pulled up the comforter, I realized I was smiling uncontrollably. Cole returned my grin.

"What just happened?" I asked Cole.

"I don't think we need to put a label on it, tonight," he said.

"No, not tonight," I said. "But we do need to get some sleep, since we both have the dinner shift tomorrow." I turned out the lamp on my bedtable and snuggled in beside him. "Cole," I whispered.

"Yes, Justin?"

"Cole," I said, and then I drifted into a deep and dreamless sleep.

Chapter Two

Sunday nights at *Civitavecchia* were busy, but not so hectic as Saturdays. I looked forward to Sundays because the pace was more measured, and then I knew I'd have Monday off. Was the menu Roman? Not exactly, but we did serve lots of fish, and we imported Italian artichokes so we could double-fry them *alla giudia*. Only those *carciofi* will do. California and France both grow wonderful artichokes, but that variety has a tough choke that will never melt the way the Italian ones do. We imported cases of them in the spring and whenever we could get them. We even blanched and froze some, so we could maintain a menu item that was as popular as any.

All year 'round we served veal dishes; a wonderful lamb shank braised in red wine with garlic and anchovy, and thin little *pizzette* that crisped quickly in a large wood-burning oven. The most popular one—at lunch, especially—was topped with wilted dandelion, crisp bits of *guanciale* (more on that later), garlic, and crumbled fresh ewe's-milk cheese. With a generous splash of olive oil, of course. I liked the menu. I thought Talbot struck a healthy balance between good, traditional cooking and modern flair that keeps millennials happy.

We had stations, of course. Everything for the broiler went to the two Mexican guys who tended that wonderful brick oven. They had two cousins who worked the lunch shift. The four of them were equally skilled—and reliable—so we always had expert coverage, even when one of them had a new baby or a death in the family or whatever sort of life event. They covered for each other. It allowed me to sleep nights.

In that same oven they roasted a half chicken that developed mahogany skin (it stayed close to the door so it could be tended and turned until it was cooked through). They produced a steak so succulent that no one would ever miss the grill marks. And a pork cutlet that was beautifully seared but still slightly rosy inside. I was especially proud of how carefully they roasted a whole fish—a *branzino* or *orata*. They knew the skin had to be beautifully blistered just as the heat reached the bone.

I rarely had to train anyone for that broiler station, because the guys trained anyone new. It was important that those dishes were always perfect when they left the kitchen. And they were, 99.9% of the time. The broiler team worked in tandem with the vegetable station, which prepped all the garnishes and sides. It was headed up, at dinner, by a frail-looking young woman who was a recent culinary school graduate. I sensed, when I hired Anna, that she was actually quite fierce. I was right. She made the station her own. And nearly everyone else in the kitchen depended on her quality work.

I never heard a catcall in my kitchen. I wouldn't have tolerated any slight directed at anyone. I demanded the same respect among team members as I demanded for myself. And I got it. On a good night—and there were many of them—the cooperation between stations was a thing of beauty. My little peaceable kingdom.

We had a pasta station, of course. Just a few things, mostly focused on vegetables and shellfish. I had hired a Chinese guy who shared his hours with his sister and their cousin. They delivered uniform results. I had suggested a *rotolo* made with saffron-infused pasta stuffed with the usual ricotta and spinach plus strips of sautéed eggplant. Talbot approved. The dish made it onto the regular menu. We found it practical for banquets and events, as well as for daily service. Talbot would never have considered anything spaghetti-and-meatballs, of course, and neither would I. Pasta was more important at lunch, but we took our dinner offerings quite seriously, too.

Cole was the new anchor for the sauté station. I learned early on that I could leave him to it—and go wherever I was needed. I often wound up expediting—sending plates out *together* for a table. I envy restaurants where the kitchen can just send things out when they're perfectly done—like *dim sum.* We were obliged to get each course on each table with each dish in perfect condition. And we mostly did it.

In the middle of it all? Little ol' me. I felt that I, like a schoolteacher, had developed eyes in the back of my head. I could sense the most minor potential train wreck. I could dash anywhere in the kitchen to pick up the slack and prevent a disaster. I had seasoned professionals all around me—as well as a steady stream of newbies—and yet I was the only one in the house who knew how to do *everything.* And *everyone* knew it. I was also the only one in the house whose job depended entirely on a smooth-running kitchen.

There were others in my team, of course. I had a minor crush on the Puerto Rican kid who, in the basement, butchered the pig we ordered every week or so. This guy was responsible for cutting out the cheeks and curing them—hence, the *guanciale* I promised to tell you about, which flavored our best-selling *pizzetta*. And he also prepared the cutlets, and then boned out the rest of the loins and the legs, of course, and garlicked and rosemaryed and rolled what would become another signature product, *porchetta!*. I thought that was probably Talbot's smartest menu choice.

Our *porchetta* was sublime, if I do say so myself. Little Luis got the salt and the garlic and the pepper and the rosemary just right, every time. And the broiler guys found the perfect position in the brick oven to roast it—slowly, carefully, attentively. They coaxed the best from the beast and the fine hand of man. The *porchetta* sandwich was the second-best seller at lunch. We had a dinner starter with a thin slice of *porchetta* accompanied by lightly pickled vegetables. It was always my first choice.

Luis found creative things for us to do with the rest of the pig, of course. He sent the bones upstairs, where we made a collagen-rich stock that we reduced and kept handy to anchor sauces. Luis once showed me how to prepare pig skin for *chicharron*—both Puerto Rican and Mexican styles. I asked him to just do it and to let me figure out a way to use it. And that's what we did. We didn't receive a lot of guts with our pigs (sausage companies need casings, after all) but we asked for the liver, and Luis did amazing things with it. The *crostini* were so much richer than what we could have made with chicken livers. And when Luis wasn't taming a pig, he was preparing pizza dough—or whatever else was needed upstairs.

I decided early in my career that I was more of a cook than a baker. So I took special care to entrust the pastry station to a fellow Johnson & Wales grad. Maggie Arundel was a year behind Scott and me, but we still got to know her, and we both fell in love with her sweet nature and her extraordinary talent. Scott and Maggie dated for a while. They made a handsome couple, but there didn't seem to be staying power in their romantic union. Their friendship, however, never wavered. J & W is famous for its pastry department, of course, but Maggie was one of those rare individuals who can absorb the wisdom of the past and then soar into a rarefied realm of their own.

The desserts Maggie created for *Civitavecchia* were stellar. They tended to get better reviews than the food did, but I was incapable of jealousy because I adored her so. And because I admired her talent so. Maggie worked with the usual ingredients: almonds, hazelnuts, chocolate (of course), lemons, blood oranges (in season), berries, and other fruits when they were at their peak—peaches, nectarines, apricots, and figs in the summer. In the fall we imported pears from Italy—the kind that taste like pears. Maggie dropped thick slices of pear into hot caramel that poached them and created a delicious syrup at the same time. A crisp little pastry case. A dollop of something custardy. Sublime.

Whatever the season, Maggie's platings were always lovely. And I never saw a plate leave her station that was not also perfectly balanced—a little rich, a little tart, a little crunch, a little hot, a little cold. Nothing was ever too sweet, just as nothing was ever bland. Maggie baked rich cakes that were perfect at 4:00 with coffee or tea, but the real genius of her list was the way her dinner offerings could tempt even the jaded, the overfed, the bored. No one ever left a morsel on one of Maggie's plates. And don't think we don't check those things.

Like all great artists, Maggie was restless enough to try strange, new combinations. I once tasted a mousse she flavored with Cynar—that odd brown artichoke sweet-and-bitter *digestivo*—which she paired with some poached fruit or other. It was lovely. Maggie had a willing accomplice in the bar manager, Alicia. Much more about her later. A well-stocked bar holds many treasures for the pastry kitchen. Maggie took advantage of the possibilities.

The only real obstacle in my kitchen was the Salad Witch. I've met far too many of these people in my career. I hope they're dying out. They're people who know where the body is buried, or who have some other leverage. I've never understood it fully. In this situation, I was trying to run a quality kitchen, and Talbot saddled me with a sour, middle-aged woman who was abusive to nearly everyone around her. But not to me, of course. She knew better.

My kitchen team learned to ignore her, as much as possible. But the servers! The house manager was a hot little guy with a perfect ass and nice ear jewelry. Roger Clemmons ran a tight ship. He was also a precious friend. I'll tell you lots more about Roger. With great pleasure. His friendship and his collaboration are still shaping my life. But I'm getting ahead of myself.

Years ago, a long-retired restaurant critic wrote a grumpy review of a dining experience, one where he had suddenly returned to the New York dining scene after a long absence. He described the entire wait staff as looking as if they had just rolled out of bed after activity that did not include sleeping. He also complained that they behaved with patrons just as they probably did with their parents: He called them sullen, evasive, monosyllabic, and bored.

Roger was careful to choose servers who were quite the opposite. They were great-looking, groomed, energized, pleasant but not pushy, and thoroughly knowledgeable about the menu. We had tastings of new dishes before each shift. I answered questions. We treated the servers with respect, and of course I demanded the same respect for my kitchen team. Everyone understood that it was a joint effort, and anyone who didn't understand that was soon out the door.

Everyone but the Salad Witch, that is. I told Roger there wasn't much I could do about her little tyrannies. I told him, "Please make sure your runners get in and out of her station with no confrontation. She's reasonably harmless when people don't engage." He understood, of course. Friction was rare. In fact, I felt more at home at *Civitavecchia* than in any other kitchen I had experienced. That was the atmosphere Cole walked into that autumn afternoon. I would have made him feel at home, too—even if I hadn't been smitten. Which I most certainly was.

📖

"Let's get a beer after," I suggested again on Sunday night.

"Sure," Cole said, as before. I began to hope it could become a nightly ritual: a glass of red; Coley in my bed. Habit-forming, no doubt. But what a sublime addiction! I questioned the wisdom of such an alliance, of course. What were the ethics concerning having an affair with my sous? I didn't much care, really. I decided I deserved all the comfort I could get. And surely no one at the restaurant—not even the Salad Witch—could give a rat's ass what Cole and I did away from work. We did our jobs—well—when we were there. After work was strictly our business. I hoped.

"The Malbec again?" I asked.

"Sounds good. I liked it," Cole said.

"And I liked *you*," I said. "Will you come home with me again? Will you come to my bed again?"

"Of course," Cole said. "But I need another history lesson. I can't very well fall in love with you if I don't know who you are."

"Are you serious, Cole?" I asked. "Could you really fall in love with me?"

"I already have, but never mind that. I'm all ears."

"You knew, didn't you?" I said. "You knew I was head-over-heels for you. You knew it was more than just wanting you because you're beautiful."

"Justin, I like it when you woo me. But I'm not getting any history."

"Quite right," I said. I paused for a minute, sipped my wine, and took a deep breath. I decided to just start speaking and see where it led: "I didn't like being a child very much. Those endless summer days when the sun didn't set until after 8:00 were pure pleasure for my neighbors and cousins. They were torture for me. I was dying to get back to school, where at least there was a chance of figuring out how to beat the odds on childhood and get on with real life.

"I didn't much like my classmates. They didn't seem to know anything. Only adults had anything to teach me, or so it seemed. I only really bonded with two other students—a girl named Mary, who was super smart, and a boy named Dennis, who was also smart, as well as breathtaking to look at. At age *six,* Dennis was a beauty, and he only got better looking as we grew up. I was madly in love with him all through our school years. Did we experiment? *Yes* would be a safe bet.

"I don't think we learned much about our bodies or our hearts when we fumbled around in Dennis's bedroom or in mine. I never questioned the fact that I was gay. I didn't know what it really meant in terms of how I could express myself. But I always knew. I think Dennis's path was different. I think he needed to try things. I think he needed to find his way, somehow. And I think he loved me almost as much as I loved him.

"But our senior year, Dennis decided on Stanford. Right after graduation he headed to California for a summer enrichment experience before the fall term. Our goodbyes were mostly of the handshake variety. And then we lost touch. I suppose I could find Dennis if I really wanted to. It's so easy to locate anyone these days. But I don't think I could face it. I don't really want to hear about his great job in Silicon Valley or about his wife and his children. I think, instead, I'll nurture the sweet memories and the dull ache at the bottom of my heart that has never left me. Never will, I expect. Mary, by the way, went to

Princeton, and now she teaches art history at Harvard. Cole, can I just leave it at that for tonight?"

"Of course, Justin," he said. "Let's get you home." And that's what we did.

Chapter Three

Waking up Monday morning with Cole in my bed was like a waking dream. If I hadn't actually felt him in my arms, I wouldn't have believed it was real. "I like the way you look in the morning," I said to him.

"I like the way _you_ look all the time," Cole answered. "_Even_ in the morning. Let me make you some breakfast."

"I don't know. Can you cook?"

"We'll find out." I gave Cole a cotton robe. I'd have preferred to see him in my good robe—the silk one—because it suited him so. But really, that's no way to cook. He headed for the kitchen. _I_ threw on the silk robe and followed him. I don't cook much at home, but I do keep staples on hand. Hey, you never know. Cole proceeded to sauté some bacon, scramble eggs, and make coffee with hot milk. I sat contentedly at my kitchen table and watched him. I loved the way he focused, effortlessly, on the task at hand. I loved the way the morning light caressed his face and his collarbones. I loved _him_, of course.

As Cole prepared our breakfast, I also thought about what was happening to the two of us. I have no illusions about being color-blind. I doubt many Americans are—color-blind, that is. I had long been attracted to black men and had enjoyed some exceptionally hot sex with some of them. I was also strongly drawn to tall, slim redheads with alabaster skin. So what? Surely my falling in love with Cole had nothing to do with his being "my type." Surely our souls met. End of story. Surely his experience was similar: Surely Cole had no preconceived attraction to white boys from Connecticut. Or was I fooling myself?

"I'm sorry you have to work tonight," I said. "It would be so much nicer to spend the whole day together."

"Let's see what we can do with the time we have," Cole suggested. And, of course, that's what we did. We shared our meal, and then we put the breakfast things into the sink.

Will you come back to bed?" I asked. Cole smiled broadly. "I love it when you smile at me, but I love it even more when you kiss me." Cole gave me his hand, and I led him to my bed. We dropped our robes and slid between the sheets—sheets that still retained a trace of overnight warmth from our bodies. "Cole, I've never felt a man's skin as silky as yours. I could lie here for hours with my arms around you. I wouldn't need anything else."

"I know the feeling, Justin. But I want more. For instance, at this moment, I want your dick in my mouth. It's my new favorite dessert."

"I just want you to be happy, Cole. Take whatever you want." And that's what he did. But not for too very long. I stopped him. "Sorry, Coley. Not yet, please. I want to hold on to the pleasure a while longer. Can you think of something else?"

"Of course." Cole started a tour of my body, pausing to explore each feature, carefully, as if he were learning it—as if he were planning to map it from memory. I'm often—not aggressive, exactly, but firm about getting what I want. Not that Monday morning. Instead, I surrendered my body to Cole, to use as he saw fit. And he did. He honored me with his warm hands and his generous mouth. He seemed to be everywhere at once.

To start, I was spread-eagle on my back while Cole explored my frontside. And then he asked me to roll over. I was happy to comply. And then I was spread-eagle on my belly while Cole toured my backside with the same care and attention as he had shown to my front. I was content to let him roam unsupervised until he developed a strong interest in my butt. I didn't exactly tense up, but I have some historical issues there.

"Justin, will you let me . . .?"

"Yes," I said. I'd have preferred "no," but I couldn't do it to him. Not to Cole. I never let guys I hooked up with go there. I never let *Jamie* go there, for God's sake. He wanted to. Sometimes. But I didn't think I could do it. I didn't think I could let even a man who loved me enter my body that way. But when Cole asked, my feelings seemed incidental. I only wanted his pleasure. Nothing else mattered to me at that moment.

"Justin, please roll back over," he said. "I want to see your beautiful green eyes. I want to kiss you. I want to be able to reach for your dick. I want to feel your balls against my body each time I go deep." I surrendered *most* of my reservations. We arranged my legs for maximum access. Cole moved into position. When he presented his exquisitely hard dick, I had only a split-second of resistance. And then I welcomed him in. "Are you okay?" he asked.

"Yes," I said. "Don't stop." Cole took me at my word. He filled my body with his. He inhabited me. I realized my body was no longer mine, but Cole's. He claimed it. He possessed it. He worshiped it. It was only the intense pleasure I felt that kept me from leaving my body. I could have been watching from my bedroom chair except that Cole inside me kept me firmly grounded to my bed.

"Sweet Jesus!" Cole shouted as he filled me with his essence. I held Cole's thighs to keep him deep. I craved whatever he could give me. Before he had finished throbbing Cole reached for me, and I was more than ready. I let loose while Cole was still filling me with his beautiful self. I shot all over both of us. And we both started to laugh. I think it was probably the most joyous moment I can remember. And I shared it with Cole.

When we were pretty much our ordinary selves again, Cole said, "Justin, I've never had an experience quite like that before. You were magnificent."

"Well, I had a good partner," I joked. "Coley, that was amazing. I don't go there, but I'm glad I did."

"So am I. Justin, I love you so much it scares me. What are we going to do about this?"

"I'm a little scared, too, Coley. But if we both continue to love each other, then I think we'll be fine."

"It's what I want," Cole said.

"What *I* want is for you to continue to help me run my kitchen smoothly, and for you to move in here and help me make a life. I haven't had much of one lately—maybe ever. I could build my life around you, if you'll have me."

"Yes, Justin."

"I don't want to pressure you, Coley, but you're welcome to move in, any time. It's not much, but it's big enough for two. I've done it. It works."

"I'm sure you're right, Justin. I have a lease. I can probably break it with a 30-day notice. I hear New York City landlords are always happy to move in new tenants and raise the rent. But I think we should maybe take our time. I don't think we have to make decisions that important today."

"Of course not, Cole," I said. "All we have to do today is love each other and be as happy as we can be, even though you have to go to work in a few hours. I'm a cruel taskmaster, I know."

"A regular Simon Legree, you mean?" he asked.

"Coley, let's not go there. Please, let's not let any negativity intrude on our love."

"You're right, Justin," Cole said. "I still have an hour or so before I have to shower. What should we do?"

"How about if we just talk for an hour or so? That way I'll get to look at you for an hour or so, too. That makes me very happy."

"What shall we talk about?" Cole asked.

"Let's talk about you. You've become my favorite topic. I want to know everything," I said.

"You want a lot," he said. "So do I. I want it all. I wasn't sure how much you'd be willing to share. Until this morning. Now, I think—I hope, anyway— that you'll open up to me." I started to get a little misty.

"I thought we were going to talk about *you*." I said.

"We *are* talking about me," Cole said. "We're talking about how much I love you. And we're talking about all the things you haven't told me about *you*,

Justin. You can't just skate along the surface and expect me to take your arm and do a pretty pirouette on cue. Life is messy. If you don't get down in it with me, then we won't have a future. I'll tell you anything. But like I said after my first day on the job, it's top-down.

"You run a great kitchen, Justin. If you can promise me the same quality in our relationship; if you can share your *soul* with me the way you shared your body just now, then I'll get up every morning and kiss the floor you walk on. But if you keep holding back, then, I don't know. I don't know what we'll have, together. I don't know how long I can wait. I've had my share of relationships that don't go anywhere. I'm not willing to do it again. I'd rather be alone."

I started to weep. Seriously. Cole reached for me. He enveloped me in his embrace and said, "Don't cry, baby. I'm here. I'm holding you. You're safe." And so I was—safe in Cole's arms. I pulled myself together, eventually.

"I'm not going to worry about whether or not I deserve you," I said. "I'm just going to see if I can earn your trust."

"I *trust* you, Justin, but I don't *know* you. And that's not good enough."

"I'll do anything, Cole. I'll dig deep. I'll tell you anything you want to know. I'll tell you things *I* don't want to know—to remember. Please don't give up on me. I couldn't bear to lose you."

"Thank you, Justin," Cole said. "I don't want to pressure you, either. But I don't want us to miss the chance to have it all. Jesus! That's too much for one Monday morning. Justy, will you have another coffee with me?"

"I thought you'd never ask," I said. We got ourselves up, traded robes, and headed back to the kitchen. I sat at my little table. Cole looked splendid in midnight-blue silk shot with constellations. It was obviously a garment that should always have been his. I vowed never to wear it again. Cole warmed milk in the microwave and served us. He joined me. "Could we be together every morning, if I get it right?" I asked.

"It's exactly what I want," Cole said. "I'll have to shower soon. Is there anything I need to know about Mondays?"

"Not really," I said. "There are no new specials to worry about tonight, and all the stations are covered. We have a lot of reservations, but nothing crazy. You'll be fine. And you can always phone me if you have any questions. I'm not going anywhere—except to the laundry room and back. I'll take my phone with me. If something wacky happens, I can be there in fifteen minutes. I'm starting to experience separation anxiety, and you haven't even left yet."

"Tell me," Cole said. He took my hands in his. We sat quietly for a while.

Eventually, I said, "Coley, we're going to do this. We're going to be together. I know it."

"Yes, Justin. We're going to do it. But first, I have to take a shower and go to work."

"I'll get you a towel. Better still, let me show you where they are. Coley, *mi casa es tu casa. Es nuestra casa, de verdad.* I need a kiss," I said. I got one. I demanded another. And then I helped Cole to be the responsible one in the family. He cleaned up and went off to work, and I went back to bed—for just a half hour. Then I got up and changed the sheets, neatened the kitchen, and gave the bathroom the once-over.

All the while I wore a very foolish grin. I know because I have mirrors, of course. And the me that stared back—when I passed one—was unlike any me I could remember. I did my chores, and then I tried to figure out how I could get through the rest of the day without Cole. I managed to survive the day alone because I wasn't *really* alone: I carried Cole in my heart, and I sensed him on my skin, in my robe, up my ass, even. Yes, Cole was a part of me. But could I keep him? I had no idea.

Chapter Four

"Cole, what made you want to cook?" I asked one weekday morning when we were sharing coffee at my kitchen table.

"I remember the exact moment I knew, actually. I woke up a little earlier than usual one morning, when I was maybe eight. I went to the kitchen, where my grandmother was making morning happen, as always. 'You look a little warm,' she said. 'Come here.' I obeyed, of course. She put her lips on my forehead, 'No fever,' she said. Grandma gave me a glass of buttermilk, to hold me over until my breakfast was ready. She said, 'Sit down, Sugar. Your food is coming soon.' She had her right hand in a bowl of flour and who-knew-what-else. I asked, 'Meemaw, what's that?' She said, 'Don't ask me unless you really want to know, Sugar, because I don't have time to answer foolish questions.'

"I didn't budge. She looked at me. She stopped her work. She took my hands in hers, and she said, 'Whoo! With hands this warm, you'll have to go like the wind to cut the lard in fast. I *hate* a greasy biscuit!' And that was my first cooking lesson. I've baked a lot of biscuits through the years. Never for you, Justin, I just realized. Maybe next Monday morning? I'd like that. I'm out of practice, but it always comes right back to me. *Meemaw* comes

"

right back to me. I'd like you to meet her. Whenever I put my hands into a biscuit bowl, she materializes."

"I'll take my chances, but I don't think she'll like me very much," I said. "I don't think she'll approve of the white kid from Connecticut who fell in love with her grandson. I don't think she'll trust me to cherish her precious boy."

"As long as *I* can trust you . . ."

"and you can,"

". . . then Meemaw will accept you, too. Ham biscuits would be fun. Do you know about country ham?"

"Not really," I answered.

It's an aged raw ham that's cured with lots of salt and pepper. Probably a little sugar, too. Most things in the South are. It doesn't come out like *prosciutto crudo*, exactly. Drier, really. And no one eats it raw, as far as I know. Country ham is sliced about 1/8-inch thick and pan-fried until it's browned. The cooking intensifies the salt, of course, so a biscuit makes a good buffer. A piece of country ham tucked inside a warm biscuit is as good as it gets, for Southerners. I think you'd like it, too."

"It sounds delicious, but where will we find country ham? I don't think my purveyors carry it."

"No, they wouldn't. It was everywhere in Georgia and the Carolinas when I was growing up, of course. It's available in DC. But north of there? Not likely. Somebody told me I could buy a whole Smithfield ham in Chinatown. But no slices. Restaurants can afford to buy whole hams. Families? Not so much. I don't know what home cooks do. Dry-cured ham is an important ingredient in various styles of Chinese cooking, of course. Maybe housewives here do without. Or maybe they stash a ham in the fridge and dole it out as needed. It keeps nearly forever, after all."

"I'm not so sure we need one stashed in our fridge," I said.

"No, Justin. We don't need a Smithfield ham in the fridge. I was thinking we should buy some slices of big pink smoked ham and pan-grill them until they're very brown. Close enough."

"That sounds fine," I said. "But I never can seem to get close enough—to you. Maybe if we were joined at the hip?"

"I think we can find better ways to get close. I think we already have. And I think I'm ready for another try. How about you?"

"I'll race you to my bed," I said. "Winner's choice."

"We're both winners, Justie. Don't you see?" Cole said. "Come, darling. Let's make love. Together. Show me what would bring you the most pleasure. I'll do anything for you, Justin. I'll do anything *with* you. As long as it isn't a competition."

Cole rendered me speechless, once again. I offered him my hand. He took it, and I led him to the bed, once again. We sank into it, once again. "I don't know whether to laugh or cry," I said as I held Cole.

"How about both?" Cole suggested. And that's mostly what I did. That wonderful Wednesday morning, with a November cold snap blanketing the Northeast and rising heat making the radiator pipes clank in my funny old apartment, I held Cole as firmly as I dared. I didn't actually show him what I most wanted, I'm sure. But he knew anyway. Cole wrapped his strong, lean legs around my waist. I reached for the perfect modeling of his butt cheeks. I hesitated long enough to be certain that I saw welcome in his eyes, and then I entered his precious body.

"Yes, Justin," he said as he accepted me. "Yes, darling, welcome home." My eyes rarely left Cole's beautiful face, and my lips rarely left *his* lips as I inhabited my beloved. I didn't *think* too much. At the time. I've been accused of over-thinking situations. Various situations. An old boyfriend said to me once, "For you, Justin, sex is not a sensual experience—it's a psychological intrigue." That was not who I wanted to be.

That November morning, Cole helped me on my way to becoming the man I most wanted to be—the *lover* I dared to be in my deepest heart. Cole surrounded me. He enveloped me. He accepted me. And he demanded my complete attention. My complete participation. My complete presence in the act of making love. That was it, really. I made love to Cole as simply and as purely as I had ever done—if indeed I had ever really made love to a man before.

My orgasm was deeply satisfying. Cole said his was, too. But that was never the goal. It was always about the two of us. It was about the shared experience. It was about our love. Nothing in my past had prepared me for the rush of feelings that washed over me. I felt drained of all negativity and pettiness. I felt fearless. I felt washed clean.

"Cole," I said, "what made you decide to take me on?"

"What do you mean?" he asked.

"You're obviously a healer, darling," I said. "You could be out there laying on hands to cure the sick and the halt. You could be in any other bed in the world, but you chose mine. You could be mending any other heart, but you decided to repair mine. Why?"

"Justin, you have such a strange sense of yourself," Cole said. "You're handsome, you're charming, you're talented, you're accomplished. Half the gay men in New York would gladly drop to their knees for the chance to service that beautiful dick of yours. And the other half would pray for the chance to get up your ass. And you're asking me why I chose you? Why not ask why *you* chose *me*?"

"Jesus, Cole! You don't let me get away with much, do you? Okay, I promise to stop asking stupid questions—as long as you promise to keep loving me."

"It's a deal," Cole said. "And maybe you'll shut up and let me kiss you." That's exactly what I did. We spent the rest of our morning in a quiet celebration of the two of us together. And then we got on with our day. Heading to work with Cole felt as light and carefree as if we were heading for a walk in the park. Surely I had never been so happy. And yet, surely the happiness was not of my making.

I didn't dwell on it, exactly, but I did wonder if I could sustain the joy in my heart. I did not have much of a history of long-term relationships, after all. I asked myself, "Justin, can you do this? Can you give Cole what he needs? What he deserves?" And I had no clear answer.

Chapter Five

I went into the dining room sometimes when service was purring along. I kept a spotless monogrammed chef's coat handy for such occasions. Even though I played second fiddle, there were customers who wanted to meet me; to express their pleasure with the dining experience; to press the flesh. I was happy to show up and be the face of the brand. Roger liked it when I swanned through the dining room. I didn't mind doing it. I'd have preferred to be cooking, but I could do the PR thing as well.

Whenever Roger came into the kitchen and said, "Chef, when you have a moment, we could use you," I always obliged as quickly as possible. I never questioned Roger's business sense. If he told me I was needed, then I showed up. When I located him in the dining room, he'd say to me, quietly, "Justin, I need a little charm at table 20. Follow me. Tell them you're sending a special little *entremets*." Or he might say, "Table 15 needs the Justin touch. I don't think you'll have to take your dick out, but be prepared, just in case." Roger knew a good bit about my dick, actually. More about that later.

Whenever I ventured into the front of the house, the bar manager, Alicia García Sánchez, tried out new cocktails on me. She was an interesting woman—a wiry little thing, deadly attractive, perfectly skilled at mixology and at organizing her staff to make our bar experience silky smooth. I'm not sure exactly where Talbot discovered her, but she turned out to be *Civitavecchia*'s secret weapon. To be fair, I have to say that Roger did a formidable job with the dining room, as well, but the two of them together made the front of the house pure gold.

I had no illusions about my indispensability. Many chefs could have come in to take my place. But who else could have done what Roger and Alicia did together? I'm sure I don't know. Alicia was also the shop foreman. I was glad there was a strong union at the restaurant. I don't think anyone in corporate management would have wanted to cross swords with her. I wondered where her skills would take her. I always suspected she was headed for politics. Time will tell.

"Will there be a place for me in the new order?" I asked one night when Alicia gave me a mysterious Campari concoction to try. It was good, but I'd have preferred a Negroni.

"There will always be a place for handsome men with good hearts," she said. "I'll grandfather you in."

"You could have maybe *brothered* me in, you know," I said. "You might find that we're closer to the same family—and the same generation—than you think. I'm just saying."

"Why, Chef!" she said. "How radical of you! I knew there was something about you I always liked. And I don't mean how great your pecs look in your whites. I'm sure they look even better *out* of your whites. But it's not that." I started to blush. Or was it the cocktail? "We need good people with us. I'm glad to know we can count on you when the time comes to make some real changes. Meanwhile, look at this bar scene!"

There were dozens of imbibers, sitting on stools at the bar and in comfy chairs at little tables. They nibbled as well. I thought Talbot's bar menu was pure genius: piquant little bites guaranteed to stave off hunger pangs (and salty enough to encourage repeat drink orders) interspersed with more substantial fare. There will always be bar patrons who want to chow down and call it dinner. We were ready for them. It was a happy crowd, but not boisterous. Alicia seemed to control the guests as easily as she controlled her handsome staff. We never had an incident at the bar. Not every restaurant can say that.

I headed to the kitchen and changed back into my service whites. "Cole," I said to him, *sotto voce*, "I want to kiss you so badly I can't think straight."

"*Oui, Chef.*" That is, after all, the only sanctioned response in a restaurant kitchen. "Perhaps later might be better," Cole suggested, quietly. And then, in full voice, he said, "I think we have enough lamb for tonight's service, but it doesn't look good for tomorrow. And Pablo just told me they blew through the inventory of whole pompanos. So you'll have to order more if you want to extend that special."

Thank you, Chef," I said. "I'll get on it." I did. I did my job. Thoroughly. We were a large enough operation to require a steward. Liz was with us from the beginning, and she set up a model that triggered reorders when anything went below a certain count—anything from milk to butter to cheeses to olive oil to fresh herbs to toilet paper for the bathrooms. But there were lots of items—meats and fish, mostly—that were my responsibility.

I'd have preferred to be cooking, but I was perfectly willing to spend a little time at my desk each day. I'll admit there was a mild thrill that accompanied ordering hundreds of dollars'-worth of the finest aged prime beef New York purveyors had to offer. The month we opened, I went to the fish market in the middle of the night most weekdays. But when I found a dealer who understood the quality we required, I started to sleep nights and place orders on the phone during business hours.

It was all part of the job. Some of it was beginning to feel stale before Cole entered my life. But the joy he brought me lightened my heart. And that lightness extended to everything I did. I was willing to waltz through the workday with a smile on my face, as long as I could be with Cole at the end of the day. And most nights he came home with me and gave me the gift of his perfect self.

📖

After a few weeks of bliss, the terror began to set in—night terror, to be exact. I began to wake with a start and then head to the bathroom to sit for a while, in the soft glow of the nightlight, until it passed. One night, after I had a particularly physical bout with the screaming meemies, Cole came out to check on me. "Justy, what's wrong?" he asked sleepily.

"I don't know, Coley. Please go back to sleep. I wouldn't have disturbed you for anything." Cole approached me and took my face in his hands. I wrapped my arms around his slim waist and buried my face in the warmth of his crotch. "I love you so much," I said.

"I love you more," Cole said. "Please come back to bed as soon as you can." I think it was at that moment, precisely, that I realized I couldn't imagine my life without Cole. What if I lost him? What if he left me? What if he got flattened by a bus? What if he got bored with me? It happens. It happens every day. I took a few deep breaths. I wondered if I could remember any meditation techniques. Eventually, the effort to remember exhausted me, and I headed back to bed and fell into a nearly comatose sleep.

"I won't push you, Justin," Cole said the next morning, "but I think you need to open up."

"I think you're right," I said, "but I can't do it on an empty stomach. Do we have any cheese?"

"Yes, Justin. There's some *taleggio*, and I took it out of the fridge last night. Let me slice some of that wonderful bread from the Essex Street Market." Within seconds Cole served me a perfect little morning feast, complete with French butter and apricot preserves. I fortified myself. I asked for another coffee. And then I went there:

"My parents were okay. They didn't beat me or starve me or anything. They encouraged me to do my homework and to brush my teeth before bed. I talk to them on the phone every week or so. I don't mind it. But I'm not certain we've known one another—then or now. Both of my folks came from small families. There were only a few cousins. Dad's sister had three children. I saw them at family gatherings, which were quiet and infrequent. The only family we interacted with regularly was my mother's brother, James, who lived next door to us with his wife, Elizabeth.

"One Saturday, Uncle Jimmy asked me to help him with a project in his garage. I was happy to do it. I steadied 2X4s while he nailed them together, for some sort of door frame, I think. We took a break. Aunt Elizabeth had brought out a pitcher of iced tea before she got into her car and went shopping. Uncle Jimmy poured. I must have been ten, at the time. Jimmy asked me, over iced tea, 'Justin, do you want to see what an adult penis looks like?' I did, of course. He opened his kakis and brought out his package.

"'You'll have one like this yourself in a few years. What do you think, Justin?' What I thought was that it was the most beautiful thing I had ever seen. 'May I touch it?' I asked. 'Of course,' he said. 'You'll never learn anything if you don't reach for it.' I did reach for it. And Uncle Jimmy's dick responded to my touch. As I held it, it grew in little throbbing beats until it was standing at full attention. 'What do you think now?' Jimmy asked. I had no answer. I simply stared at it in awe. And I continued to hold it.

"I had already discovered masturbation, when I was about six. But the process only produced intense feelings, with no physical evidence. I had no idea where Jimmy and I were headed. But I suspected something interesting was about to happen, and I wasn't going to chicken out. Jimmy was very calm and still, except for his breathing, which became louder. And then he said, 'Get ready for this.' The head of his dick began to squirt a surprise substance that looked hot, white, and sticky.

"'What do you think now, Justin?' he asked. 'You'll have that too, some day.' I was grateful for the lesson. Some of the ones that followed, on subsequent Saturday afternoons, were less welcome. Some of it hurt. Some of it tested my gag reflex. Some of it seemed aggressive, almost violent. But I participated. I never said no to Uncle Jimmy, no matter what he wanted from me.

"He never swore me to secrecy. Not exactly. He just made it clear, from our first encounter, that what happened between us in his garage was strictly between the two of us. And that no one else could know about it. Uncle Jimmy said that if I told anyone about our lessons, then they would have to stop. That was the perfect strategy to use on the ten-year-old in his thrall.

"Not only was I desperate for knowledge and experience, but I rather liked the idea of something special and private between us that no one else knew about. The lessons went on for three years, maybe? Four, probably. He carefully monitored my puberty. He congratulated me when I sprouted crotch hairs and a few whiskers. It probably made me feel proud. I was certainly not getting that kind of feedback from my father.

"As my dick began to grow, Uncle Jimmy began to treat me with a new respect, as if I were actually a young man—which I'm certain I was not. The last year, Jimmy began to ask me to top him. I did it, of course: Fourteen-year-old boys can stick it anywhere and get off fast. It was probably near my fifteenth birthday that I just couldn't do it anymore.

"I was about to start high school, and Dennis and I were becoming closer. I tried to use what I had learned from Uncle Jimmy. And yet not much of it seemed to apply—anywhere in my life. My world began to feel quite different. And one day, I looked at Uncle Jimmy and saw a sweaty old man. And I no longer wanted to be a party to our lessons.

"There was no backlash. What could he have said or done? I still see these people—but rarely. I never told anyone what was going on—not even Dennis. And neither my parents nor Aunt Elizabeth said a word about what was happening. Did they know? They aren't stupid people. Somebody must have noticed. And yet? Silence. And the silence remained until this morning. I couldn't have spoken to anyone about these things but you, Cole."

"Justin, I'm not certain you understand how deep those experiences were," Cole said. "You're an incest survivor, Justin. That makes you vulnerable and invincibly strong, all at the same time. I'm starting to know you, finally. And I couldn't love you more if I tried."

"Jesus, Coley," I said, "you're going to make me cry."

"You mean the way you never cried after Uncle Jimmy abused you?"

"I think you're right," I said. "I don't remember shedding a single tear, not even after he tore up my asshole. Jimmy was careful never to leave marks on my body that my parents could see. But they weren't proctologists, after all."

"Justy, will you let me make love to you?" Cole asked. "It's what I want most."

"Yes, Cole," I said. "It's what I want, too." Did I worry about offering Cole damaged goods? Of course. But I never verbalized it. And that morning I began to think that perhaps I could be whole, in time, with Cole's help. I wanted to heal, maybe for the first time. I wanted my heart to normalize. I wanted to be one of the men who can love and be loved without limitations. Without conditions. Without baggage. Without fear. But really, at age thirty-six, how much healing was possible?

Chapter Six

The following week, Cole and I were sitting at my little kitchen table one morning, as usual. I sat quietly with Cole across from me—warming my morning almost as if he were the sun itself and not just a beautiful reflector of its rays. I decided Cole was a planet—that's what he was: a perfect celestial body with me in his orbit.

"Talk to me, darling," I said.

"I love talking to you, Justy. What would you like to hear?"

"Look, Coley, I didn't grow up black in the South, so I don't know what to ask you. But I want to know everything you'll share with me. I feel I've met your grandmother. But otherwise, I don't know much."

"I think childhood is mostly a dirty trick," Cole said. "I doubt anyone gets off scot-free (whatever that means). You certainly didn't, and neither did I. I stopped complaining years ago. But I asked *you* to open up, and you did it. So I'll do the same. Another coffee?"

"Yes, please."

"Meemaw led a very structured existence. Her first-born didn't take to the discipline, by all reports. I only saw my mother a few times. She was sweet and pretty. And she made me laugh. But she had nothing else to offer me. Meemaw took me in the day

I was born, I'm told. And when my mother felt recovered from the delivery, she moved to Savannah to start a new life.

"No one ever spoke about my father. I think Meemaw knew who he was. I think. She wouldn't say. And since he was permanently absent from my life, I didn't dwell on him. I wondered, of course. I might have gotten some answers from my grandpa, but he died just before my fifth birthday. Meemaw was inconsolable for the first month after my grandfather's death. But she found strength in her faith, and she got back into life.

"When I was about sixteen, I took a real interest in meeting my father. I even considered going to Savannah to confront Momma and get an answer. My Aunt Helen talked me out of it. Nice lady. She looked a lot like Momma, but they were quite different, otherwise. Unlike her older sister, Helen finished high school and married a nice guy with a job. They had two children, and they go to church every Sunday. I love my Uncle Wilbur, too. I'm a few years older than their kids. I keep in touch with all of them, occasionally—mostly at holiday time. But I haven't been back to see them since Meemaw died.

"When I started making noises about finding my father, Aunt Helen said, 'He won't never be your daddy, Sugar. Let it go.' I couldn't argue with that. I did let go. After some tears, of course. Instead, I focused on getting good grades in high school and getting out of that town." We nursed our coffees. I was silent. And then Cole said, "Do you want to ask me if white boys took me to the side of a country road and beat the shit out of me? Just because they wanted to? Just because they felt they could?"

"Stop, Coley," I said. "I can't bear to think of you in pain."

"If this is too much for you, Justin, then tell me. And maybe we'll discuss it another time. Or maybe not." I got up from the table so quickly that I sent coffee splashing everywhere. I grabbed Cole and wrapped my arms around him. I held him as tightly as I dared for several minutes.

"I can deal with anything as long as I have you in my arms," I said. Cole seemed to relax into my embrace. "Would you share an omelet with me?"

"Sure," Cole said. I released him from my grip just long enough to put a pan on the stove and to get some eggs and butter from the fridge. Then I grabbed him again. "I'm not seeing much progress," Cole said. "Do you know how to do this?"

"I used to," I said. "And then you walked into my life—and into my bed, and into my heart—and now everything's different." I eased my grip on Cole's torso. He smiled. I got to work. One of the beauties of a good omelet is that including preheating the pan and cracking the eggs, it's about a two-minute process. And that gave Cole just enough time to clean up my coffee spill and set the table.

I smiled a lot as we shared my perfect omelet. Cole smiled, too. "Jesus, Coley," I said. "You make me so happy."

"Ditto," he said.

"Please don't give up on me. I want to know everything."

Cole looked at me quizzically for a moment, and then he said, "I have a dream."

"Sorry, Coley, I think that's taken."

"Quite right, Justin. But I do have one. I'm not ready to say it out loud, even to you. But when I am,

you'll be the first to know. And I hope you'll share it.
I'm going to shut up. I don't want to tease you."

"Will you make love to me instead?" I asked.

"With the greatest pleasure," Cole said. And
that's what we did.

The next week was a busy one. There were some
private parties and other events that pushed the
kitchen to its production limits. By Sunday night,
we were all feeling the pressure. When Cole and I
headed home, together, I was more than ready for a
quiet wind-down that included red wine and Cole in
my arms.

"Justy, you're exhausted," Cole said. "Come to
the kitchen with me." I obeyed, of course. Cole sat
me down and poured a glass of red. He also poured
a shot of cognac for each of us. "Sit here and let me
see what I can do with that tangle of sinews that used
to be your beautiful shoulders. You'll never get to
sleep in this state." Again, I obeyed. Cole got to work
on me with his strong, warm hands. He was right.
My muscles were clenched in knots that were painful
when Cole untied them.

Still I slipped into an alternate state of conscious-
ness as Cole worked my shoulders. "You make a
great body servant," I said.

"What?" he asked.

"You know, in SPARTACUS when Laurence Olivier says to Tony Curtis, 'You shall be my body
servant.'"

"Justin, you're talking about slavery."

"I'm talking about Hollywood, darling," I said.

"So, do you have some favorite quotes from *GONE WITH THE WIND* to share as well?"

"Coley, please. I don't want to argue with you."

"No, and I don't want to argue with you, either, Justin. That's why I'm leaving." Cole headed to the bedroom and started packing his things. I followed, of course. Cole still had his own apartment, so he had a place to go—if indeed he really intended to desert me. Cole kept only a few outfits and some toiletries at my place. He was packed in minutes.

"I wish I understood you, Coley," I said. "I wish I could convince you to change your mind and stay here where you belong."

Cole said to me, "I thought you were different, Justin. I should have known better. My old granny warned me. When I was in high school, I met a white boy who lived on the other side of town. He was a beautiful kid. He looked maybe a little bit like you, Justin—maybe. We became boyfriends, on the down low. He was very sweet, most of the time. But not when he broke up with me. I thought I was going to die. Meemaw knew what was going on. She didn't miss much.

"She sat on the sofa and invited me to put my head in her lap, just as I did when I was a little boy. She held me and massaged my temples. Like the old days. She said to me, 'They can't help it, Sugar. It's their way.' She was a tough old bird, my granny. And I'll always be grateful for her wisdom. I just hoped maybe things had changed. Apparently not, Justin. Goodbye."

I felt as if I'd just been kicked in the gut. Not only was my love deserting me, but he also called me a racist. I guess. I wasn't certain. "Please stay, Cole. You're all I want. I thought we were building a life together. I love you. Please don't go. If I've been an asshole, then I'll fix it. Cole, I can fix anything if I have you beside me. Cole, look at me. What's happening to us?"

He did look at me. And he said, "Justin, you can fix anything in your kitchen. This is different. I love you, too. You know that. I don't think there's ever been a question about our feelings for each other. But your love for me isn't good enough. I hoped it would be. I was wrong. Let me go." He headed for the door with his small suitcase wheeling behind him. I dashed forward to stop his exit. I pinned him against my front door, really.

I wrapped my arms around him and said, "Cole, don't do this. I've known since almost the first moment we met that we belong together. I've never questioned it, not even for a millisecond. I'll do anything to keep you here. Anything short of murder. Cole, please let me put things right. Please stay." He turned and kissed me deeply, and then he was out the door.

I felt numb, at first. But when the reality of Cole's departure finally sank in, I broke into a cold sweat. I paced the floor, trying to analyze the situation and plan a strategy for getting Cole back. After about a half hour of pacing—which included a stubbed toe and a brush with the table that supported my favorite piece of art glass—I allowed exhaustion to take me over. I headed for the bedroom, stripped, and dropped into bed, without the benefit of so much as a toothbrush. I slept.

Chapter Seven

The sunrise brought with it a keen sense of loss. Monday morning signaled that I would have the whole day to wallow in my pain, without even the distraction of going to work and getting caught up in my duties. Even making coffee felt like a challenge. I sat for over an hour at my kitchen table before I sought the first morsel of food. That's not like me: I'm normally a nibbler as soon as I get up. Not that morning. And there didn't seem to be any more pleasure than appetite in my life.

I phoned the restaurant at 10:00 to tell Scott about some specials and some special needs. Not only did Scott's team pound out a perfect lunch, but they also did much of the prep for our dinner shift. I didn't say a word about Cole. I knew Cole would show up on time and helm Monday dinner just as he had been doing for weeks. All I did say was, "Thanks, Scotty. I'll probably see you tomorrow before you leave. And if not, then enjoy your Wednesday off. You've earned it."

And then I returned to feeling sorry for myself. I alternated self-pity with soul-searching. Cole was so smart—intellectually and emotionally—that if I had said something to offend him, it must have been an offensive remark. I searched my head and my heart. It took a while for me to analyze my insensitivity, but eventually I got it. I realized that making a joke to Cole about enslavement—no matter how innocently—proved that my heart was not so pure as I thought.

I poured a glass of chardonnay. I'm not much of a daytime drinker, but I made an exception that Monday. I sat for a while longer, thinking and sipping my wine. And then I started to cry. It was the emptiness, really. And the uncertainty. I could have accepted doing without Cole for days—even weeks—if I knew he would return. But since I lacked the luxury of that kind of certainty, I had no intention of accepting his exit. Reality would have to wait for another day.

I took a nap. I skipped laundry and other chores. I do have extra sheets and towels, after all, and plenty of shorts and socks. Who decided that laundry should be weekly? Fuck it! I watched some television, drank some more wine, took another nap. And then I ordered in a pizza for supper. It was the most miserable day off I could remember. And when I headed to bed, that was rather miserable, too. I lay there—minus the warmth of Cole's body beside me—and stared up at the darkened ceiling or at the tiny gap in the armor of my window shade that insisted on admitting a glimmer of street light.

Eventually, I adopted some Scarlett O'Hara philosophy: I told myself, "I've just got to get him back. Well, I won't think about that now. I'll think about that tomorrow. After all, tomorrow is another day." So Cole was right. So my heart was rooted in another era—not-a pretty era at that. I was disgusted. And exhausted. I slept.

I got in a little early on Tuesday, as I often did. Scott was still in the middle of a flawless lunch service, as usual. I went to my desk and started to pound out the orders and stomp out the brush fires that sprang up over the weekend, as usual. Scott popped into my office, as they were nearing the end of service, to give me an update, as usual. He took one look at me and said, "Justin, you look like shit. What's going on?"

"Cole left me," I said.

"Sorry to hear it, buddy. I thought you two were meant for each other."

"So did I," I said. "But I fucked up. I can't talk about it."

"I have an available shoulder for crying on, but not too late at night. We start our prep at 7:00 AM, you know. Look, Justin, without even trying, I'll bet I could find at least a dozen hot women who'd be happy to fuck you till you're blind. I'm just saying."

"Thanks, Scotty," I said as I embraced him. "But I don't want a dozen hot women. I want Cole."

"Well, then fix it, Justin. You're a good man. And a smart man. Fix it."

"I'm going to try," I said.

"Look, Justin," Scott said, "it's been obvious to me every time I've seen Cole that he worships you. That doesn't change overnight. Justin, don't shut down! You have work to do. But it's none of my business."

"What happens in my life will always be your business, Scotty, as long as you give me the gift of having you in it. Thanks for the kick in the ass. I feel better already."

"Are we cool on the business front for today?" Scott asked.

"I think so."

"I almost forgot to tell you—Jenny's pregnant!" I leapt to my feet and embraced Scott.

I said, "Scotty, I can't imagine better news! You must be bursting!"

"Pretty much. Jenny isn't ready to announce anything, but I asked if I could tell you. She said, 'Yes, but only Justin.'"

"I'm honored," I said. "Look, Scotty, I have some expectations here—beyond a healthy delivery. Please tell Jenny I expect this one to be named after me. No excuses. Justina is a nice name, too."

"I'll tell her," Scott said. "And I expect she'll be delighted."

"Good," I said. "Get out of here. Go home and give your beautiful wife a big kiss for me." The rest of the workday was less newsworthy. It was mostly about the usual chores. I dreaded seeing Cole, of course. But we both know how to be businesslike. I can always do my job—even with a broken heart.

"Chef," Cole said to me when I first saw him—my first glimpse of him since I watched him walk out on me, "I can't serve this veal. It's tough and stringy. I've had to pull it. It's on 86 at the moment. How do you want to deal with this?"

"I'll phone DeBragga right now," I said. "They may be able to send over a replacement this evening. And if not, we'll have to do without until tomorrow. I'll let you know." It's always something. I went back to my office and made the call to my most important meat purveyor. My account manager had left for the day, but they know us there. Someone else jumped in and offered to drop off a few pounds of veal leg on his way home. In the restaurant business, loyalty is often rewarded.

I told Cole what to expect, of course. And I dashed downstairs to ask Luis to stay late and trim the veal for service. He knew how to clean it, slice it, portion it, and pound it just as well as Cole and I did. We would be fine. Staple menu items would be available. I could breathe a little easier. The rest of the dinner shift felt routine. It was going home alone that was the challenge.

Maggie stopped by my station at the end of service. She took one look at me and one look at Cole and said, "Chef, do you have a minute?" I suggested my office. She followed me there, and I shut the door behind us.

"Yes, Maggie. What can I do for you?"

"I wanted to talk to you about winter specials, but that can wait until tomorrow. What's going on?"

"Am I that transparent?" I asked.

"To those who love you, yes. I'm waiting."

"Cole left me," I said quietly.

"Fuck! Justin, what did you do to that beautiful man?"

"Maggie, please don't beat up on me," I said. "I feel bad enough as it is. I got it wrong. That's all I can tell you tonight."

"Come here, dear," she said. Maggie took me in her arms and held me tenderly. "How many times have we cried on each other's shoulder?" she asked. "How many beaux—and belles—have you seen me through? When you survived Jamie, I thought maybe . . . well. Now what?"

"Maggie, I have to get him back."

"Well, then you will." Maggie put her hand on my cheek. It was the same gentle hand that could wrangle a huge Hobart bowl full of batter or apply the most delicate wisp of garnish to an ethereal little pastry. She said, "Love is a powerful force for good in the world. Never forget that. Get some sleep, Justin. You obviously need it. Why don't you take me to breakfast? On Friday?"

"I'd like that," I said. "I'll text you." Maggie kissed me lightly and then headed home. Her kiss reminded me of the night, in our student days, when we tumbled into bed together after far too many glasses of wine. It didn't really go very far. I had been to bed with maybe two women before. It was fun, but I knew better than to think it was my future. Maggie was still undecided then, I think. But that silly night together cemented our friendship, somehow. And my life has always been better for it.

Roger stopped by my office after dinner service. He said, "Justin, are you going to tell me what's wrong, or are you going to make me guess?"

"You don't miss much, Roger," I said. "Do you have time for a drink?"

"Sure," he said. He looked a bit quizzical, but he didn't ask the question: the *Why aren't you going home with Cole?* question. Instead, he said, "I'll wait for you outside." When I had locked up, Roger was waiting, as promised. It was a bitterly cold night but so still that the air felt crystalline. I put on gloves, and we walked to a bar with the crunch of refrozen snow beneath our feet. It was the same bar where Cole and I first got to know each other. It was convenient. It was welcoming. And I couldn't avoid it just because of old associations. Could I?

We ordered Scotch, and once our drinks arrived and the first sips were taken, Roger said, "Whenever you're ready."

"Thanks for your patience, Roger," I said. "The truth is—Cole left me."

"Jesus, Justin!" Roger said. "What the fuck happened?"

"It's all my fault, Roger, and I can't talk about it. Not tonight. I'm too raw."

"I won't push you," Roger said. "But don't marinate in this. Don't make it worse."

"Thanks, Roger. You're too good to me."

"Justin, do you have the slightest idea how much I love you?"

"Jesus, Roger, why do you talk to me that way?"

"Because I'm a big believer in the truth. And you used to be, too," Roger said.

"*Touché.* Roger, you know how much I love you, and why," I said.

"Look, Justin, I'd love to take you home and put you to bed, but I have a million things to do in the morning. My sister Rachel gets in from LA, among other things. She adores you, you know. You have to find some time for her this week."

"I will," I said.

"Look, Justin," he said,"it's getting so late. Would you meet me in the bar tomorrow between services? 4:00? That might be our best chance to talk."

"Sure, Roger," I said. I wondered if I'd have a logical explanation for Cole's departure by 4:00 tomorrow. I wondered if I'd ever have one.

"You look beat, Justin," Roger said. "I want you to go home. Why don't you leave your knife roll with me tonight?"

"Ha, ha, ha!" I said. "Roger, I'm perfectly safe around sharp objects, as always. But thanks for your concern. Sleep well, my dear." We parted. I walked home rather slowly. Had it been windy, I'd have wrapped my scarf around my face and sprinted home. Or taken a cab. But it was such a beautiful, starry night that I needed to savor it. When I let myself into my empty apartment and bolted the door behind me, I was nearly resigned to the emptiness. Nearly.

Chapter Eight

Sitting at my kitchen table the next morning, I smiled as I thought of my scheduled meeting with Roger in the afternoon. He was a perfect *confidant,* after all. I also smiled as I remembered our history: I met Roger my first day at *Civitavecchia.* Three years earlier? No, nearly four. It was also Roger's first day, I think. The restaurant was set to open in two weeks, and we both had to whip our respective departments into shape.

I told you what a hot little man Roger is. We had instant chemistry. That was obvious to both of us. Probably to others, as well: Kitchen pants are loose enough that unwelcome erections are not all that visible—with a jacket over them, anyway. Roger's tight trousers afforded him no such disguise. But we got on with our work. After our second day, I suggested a drink. Roger accepted.

We walked to a bar—the same bar where Roger and I began to have drinks occasionally and where Cole and I fell in love, of course. That one. We had a glass of wine. Roger seemed restless. "Your place or mine?" he asked with a wonderful big smile.

"Mine, I think," I said.

"Good," Roger said. "Let's do it." We found a taxi and got home quickly. We dropped our coats on the chair by the door and headed for the kitchen. I poured two cognacs, and then I kissed Roger. He kissed me back. So far so good. I started to unbutton his shirt. His chest was even handsomer than I had imagined, and his nipple rings were impressively large. I caressed him and nuzzled him. My lips met one of his ample nipples. I ran my tongue all around it. I took his nipple into my mouth, along with the jewelry, of course.

"Bite it," he said. I nibbled playfully. "No, *bite* it," Roger said. I did my best to oblige. Then I suggested we head to my bedroom. Roger agreed. We stripped quickly, and Roger sank to his knees before me. "I knew you'd have a great dick," he said, and he proceeded to devour it. Aggressively, I thought. I wasn't used to feeling like fresh meat. But I didn't dislike it, exactly. When I sensed it was time to move on, I took Roger by his shoulders and lifted him to his feet. I kissed him, savoring the mouth that had just been consuming my dick. And then I picked Roger up and deposited him in the middle of my bed.

Roger's ass was even more luscious bare than it appeared in his trousers. I spread his legs and went for the sweet spot. He urged me on. I'd have been content to stay there for hours, except that Roger said, "Fuck me! I want your big cock up my ass, and I want it now." I couldn't argue with that. I did as I was told. I grabbed Rogers legs and pulled him to me. Within seconds I was in.

There was no question of, "Are you ready?" or "Is this okay?" It was just my dick up Roger's hole, as deeply as possible. "Harder," he demanded. "Tear it up, big boy." I did my best to respond to the situation. I pounded Roger as hard as I dared. And I'll admit it was exciting. It wasn't all that long before I found myself announcing my impending orgasm.

"Do it! Fill me up!" he said. And I gave Roger my best shot.

When I had recovered and my erection had started to flag, Roger said, "Give me your hand." I knew that was not an invitation to dance. Roger placed me where he wanted me. I had my right hand all the way up Roger's ass when he came. Hard. "Don't take it out," he commanded. "I'll tell you when." I didn't mind, really, being held captive with my hand up Roger's ass. It was a warm, pretty place to be. After about ten minutes, he said, "Pull it out." I eased my hand, slowly, from its new glove. Roger seemed disappointed that I had been so gentle with him.

The previous half hour had seemed like a roller-coaster ride. I suggested that we head back to the kitchen and finish our cognac. Roger agreed. We sat quietly for a bit. I was the one to break the silence: "I don't think I can do this," I said. "I don't think I can give you what you need."

"No, I don't think you can," Roger said. "But I'm glad we tried it. You're a beautiful man, Justin. I think I could fall in love with you, if you're willing to take me on—as a friend."

"I think we're already friends, Roger," I said, "and I think our friendship will continue to grow. Will you sleep over?"

"Not tonight," Roger said. "I have a million things to do in the morning. Promise you'll ask me again."

"Promise." Roger and I hadn't gotten to that sleepover. There was always something else press-ing—like his boyfriend or mine. And years went by— as they will. I always felt close to Roger. But I rarely saw him out of business hours. I was pleased he offered to meet with me. And I sensed some wisdom might come of it.

"You don't have to tell me anything, Justin, but I think it would do you good," Roger said as we sipped wine spritzers in a cozy corner of Alicia's bar.

"I'm sure you're right," I said. "I haven't verbalized it. I'm not certain I can do it, but I'll try." Roger smiled patiently. I took a deep breath. "Last Sunday night, Cole was massaging my shoulders after we got home from work. I told him he made a good body servant—you know: *SPARTACUS*; Laurence Olivier and Tony Curtis. I thought it was an innocent jest. Cole told me I was joking about slavery and that he was leaving me."

"What do you think now?" Roger asked.

"Yes, well, I've had plenty of time—alone—to try and work that out. I think Cole is firmly rooted in reality, and I've never known him to be hypersensitive. If he says I got it wrong, then I have no choice but to accept that."

"And now what?" Roger asked.

"I've already dug deep. I don't think I've missed any corners of my heart—none that are accessible, anyway. And of course, Cole was right: I think I've been harboring a touch of typical American institutionalized racism without even knowing it. I hate that I found it, but I can't deny it."

"Justin, don't beat up on yourself. That won't help anybody," Roger said.

"The worst of it, Roger, is that Cole told me my love isn't good enough." I misted over. Had I been anywhere other than at work, I'd have slipped into major tears.

"Justin, you're a good man with an excellent heart. If there are defects, you can fix them."

"Cole says I can fix anything in my kitchen, but that this is different," I said.

Roger said, "Cole has uncanny clarity about life, but I think he's wrong on this point: I think you *can* fix anything. I think you already have."

"Jesus, Roger!" I said. "I'm so desperately unhappy without him. Do you think I can get Cole back?"

"I do, actually," Roger said. "I'd like to help."

"You already have," I said.

"Let's talk again in a few days," Roger said. "If you haven't already figured it out, then we'll create a plan: Operation Reunion."

"Thanks, Roger. I'm sure you have things to do. I'm going back to work. I feel a little better. I love you, Roger."

"My, my, fraternization during business hours. What would management say?"

"Luckily we have the shop foreman on our side. I think we'll survive." Roger and I parted and got on with our separate but entwined evenings. I did feel a little better. I almost felt absolved. Almost.

_______ *Chapter Nine*

When I got home from work the next night, I felt so empty that I opened Grindr on my phone. I had the app from the previous year. I had only used it a few times, after Jamie left me. I didn't find the hookups very satisfying, but I preferred them to be-ing alone. If I hadn't felt so desperately lonely—and guilty, of course—I'd never have gone there. I checked out the available hookups. The one that caught my eye was a big, hot black guy who billed himself as, "aggressive top, huge dick, you won't be disappointed. I can host." He included the usual safety detail about PrEP. I sent him my profile. He accepted. I was both titillated and horrified that I had agreed to go out into the night in search of hu-miliation.

Surely I deserved it, and yet, surely I could have found a healthier way to atone for my sins. I don't do extreme things. Or at least I hadn't yet. Nothing really kinky. Nothing really dangerous. And yet, I was willing to take a risk. I was rather on autopilot as I made my way to his building. Leave it to Grindr to serve up nearby contacts first. The East Village is prime territory for hot men. I was there in about ten minutes. If the trip had taken *twenty* minutes, I might have had time to back out. But as it was? I rang his bell.

"Jesse," he said, as he extended his large, warm hand.

"Justin," I said as I shook it.

That was mostly the extent of our greeting. I'm sure he smiled. I'm not so sure I returned his smile. Jesse led me to his bedroom. It was rather dark. It contained a bed, and that was the only important fixture, after all. We stripped. He kissed me. "Great ass," he said. "And you have a nice dick, for a white boy. Maybe I'll suck it later. It depends on how good you are."

Jesse directed me to lie belly-down on his bed. That was what I came for, after all. I was resigned. What followed felt more tender than aggressive. Jesse stroked me, and he embraced me, and he rimmed me with real zeal. I'd have been content to stay with that for another hour or so. But then he moved into position to top me. I hadn't a clue what Jesse really wanted. Did he want to hurt me? Did he want to possess me? Did he want to share some sort of experience with me? Or was the whole thing just mechanics?

When Jesse presented his dick at my backdoor, I was ready. More or less. He was just as huge as advertised. I've known for years that acceptance is the key to survival. I accepted Jesse. He was in, and he went so deep I wondered if that dick of his was maybe pushing at my tonsils. I practiced deep breathing. I felt Jesse inhabiting my body. I welcomed him. I was spread-eagle on his bed, and he took full possession of me—inside and out. He placed his limbs on mine and warmed me totally. Jesse owned me, really, and I was happy to be his possession.

After what felt like an eternity, Jesse flipped me over and placed my legs on his shoulders. He eased that amazing tool of his back inside. I gasped, but I accepted it, of course. That was our contract. "Come for your daddy," he said. "Come all over your chest just because I'm filling you up deeper than you've ever been filled." His strokes were slow and even. And deep, of course. Deeper than any man I'd ever taken? Definitely. I surrendered. Totally. Jesse bent his torso forward, like a great dark tent over my body. Like protection. Like a guardian angel. I reached for him. I drew his mouth to mine. He kissed me almost as deeply as he was fucking me. It was his mouth that pushed me over the edge, I think. And then I let go. I gave Jesse what he requested. I came hard.

I continued to hold him, and to kiss him. Jesse paused while I was still throbbing. He let my body grip his amazing dick with each spasm. And when I was no longer anything but a mass of heavy breathing, Jesse gripped my shoulders and went even deeper, it seemed. Three strokes, tops, and he was a volcano. I knew it. I felt every drop. I received it as it was intended, I think: as a gift. The best Jesse had to offer, I think. I just didn't understand exactly what he intended to give, and what he had taken from me, in return.

"Justin, do you want a beer, or something?"

"I'll take a *shot* of something. But then I really have to get home." Jesse poured us some tequila. We downed our shots. We smiled. Jesse was easy and relaxed. He was gentle. I went to him in search of humiliation and atonement, and there I was sharing not just a drink but an afterglow.

"Will I see you again?" Jesse asked.

"I don't know," I said. "I think you're amazing, but I don't really hook up with guys these days. I work long hours. I needed to see you tonight, but if I can get my boyfriend back, then I'll never go on an app again."

"Justin, I think you're a beautiful man. I could get really interested in you. If you change your mind, phone me some time. Or text me once in a while. If you just want to come over and play, that's good. If you want more, that's even better. Your call."

"You'll hear from me," I said. And I meant it. "Jesse, who are you? Not that it's any of my business."

"It *could* be your business, Justin. If you want it. Let me know. My life could be an open book. But only if you really want to read it."

"I thought you wanted to hurt me," I said. "I thought I deserved to be hurt. That's why I came here tonight. Instead, you made love to me. Or so it felt."

"Yes. You got that right," Jesse said. "Maybe I have some demons of my own. Maybe mine tell me to hurt because I've been hurt. Maybe I need to make a hot white boy my bitch sometimes. And maybe your demons and mine got together and decided on a different plan. Another shot?"

"Yes, please." He poured. We downed.

"Justin, I'm serious: I'd love to see you again. I'd also love for you to stay over. I want you in my bed. No pressure. Will you consider it? I'm working from home tomorrow, so I don't have to be up at any particular hour. I have coffee. I make a mean soft-boiled egg. What do you say?"

"Jesus, Jesse!" I said. "You don't make it easy to refuse you."

"Justin, let's not play any games tonight. We've been pretty honest with each other, so far, more or less, I think. Will you stay?"

"Yes."

"Good. What time should I set the alarm for?"

"How about ten o'clock?

"Ten it is. I have an extra toothbrush. Come with me." Jesse led me to his bathroom, which was mostly black—with red towels. A little extreme but interesting. We brushed our teeth. Jesse plugged in a little night-light. "Just in case you need it," he said. I followed him to his kitchen, where he took two bottles of Poland Spring from the fridge. And then we returned to Jesse's bedroom. "Is the left side okay with you?" he asked.

"Sure," I said. I don't think guests should be too choosey. We lay down, and Jesse pulled up the comforter. He turned out the light. He reached for me, wrapped his arms firmly around me, and kissed me deeply. I kissed him back. I could feel his amazing dick against my belly, and I rose to the occasion, too. If it hadn't been three in the morning, who knows what might have happened?

"You need some sleep," he said. "Roll over." I did as I was told. Jesse spooned me and wrapped his left arm around my torso. I felt warm and perfectly safe. "Daddy's here," he whispered in my ear. "Daddy's holding his precious boy. Daddy's going to make everything right." I believed him, actually. Or at least I wanted to believe that this extraordinary hunk could make positive changes in my life. He kissed my neck and said, "Sleep well, my pretty boy." And, again, I did as I was told.

Jesse was up before the alarm jangled me awake. I was surprised that the smell of freshly brewed coffee hadn't wakened me sooner. Jesse threw me a robe. As I slipped it on, I realized he had been wearing the robe, recently. I felt his warmth, and I drew in his scent. He smelled of tobacco—not smoke, but the caramelized leaf—and something sweeter as well. Not jasmine or rose—not that floral—but something like a combination of mango and vanilla. Heady stuff.

I joined Jesse at his small dining table. "Do you always look this good in the morning?" he asked.

"I try to please," I said.

"I'll bet you do," Jesse said. "Will two eggs do it? I have plenty."

"Two sounds perfect," I said. I sipped my coffee. Jesse served me two three-and-a-half-minute eggs, just the way I like them. The toast was warm. The butter was Irish, I guessed. It was lovely. "You were right about your egg skills. I could use you at the restaurant."

"He speaks!" Jesse said. "I had given up on hearing anything about you."

I smiled and said, "I'm the chef at a restaurant you may have heard of. It's not mine."

"I'll bet you run a tight ship. If it's as tight as your asshole, then you must be doing everything right."

"Thanks for the compliment. I guess. Jesse, you still haven't told me who you are."

"I advocate for the poor and the homeless," Jesse said. "So you know there's plenty to keep me busy in this town."

"Tell me more," I said.

"Next time," he said. "When do you have to leave, Justin?"

"Noon is good."

"Excellent. That gives us a little time. Will you come back to bed, Justin? I want you there."

"Yes," I said. And that's what we did. Our second encounter was gentler and less hurried than the night before. We explored. I hadn't really noticed Jesse's beard the first times he kissed me. I liked the feel of it on my face. And it was exceptionally handsome, as was the rest of him. I enjoyed every inch of it. And speaking of inches, savoring Jesse's dick was a challenge. I did my best. I was a little more successful at honoring his balls. They were large, but I could get them in my mouth—one at a time, of course.

"Justin, I don't know how you feel about letting me in again. You can say no, of course."

"The answer is yes," I said. "But could I be on top?"

"You can be wherever you want to be, baby. As long as you'll be with your daddy." I straddled Jesse and carefully aimed him toward my interior. It was more difficult accepting him than it had been the night before, when I was expecting to be violated. But we were in no rush, after all. Eventually I relaxed enough to receive Jesse—just the head at first, and then I lowered my body onto his and slid the whole magnificent thing inside me, until I was seated firmly on his pubic bone.

I threw back my head and whooped. Jesse started to laugh. "Are you okay, baby?" he asked.

"I'm perfect," I said.

"Yes, you are perfect," he said. "Come to Daddy." I leaned forward and rested my chest on his. Jesse put his arms around me and kissed me. "Good boy," he said. "I'd never hurt my pretty boy." He began to move inside me—slowly, gently, rhythmically. And all the while he continued to embrace and pet me. And he kissed me often. I was in a state of bliss. I'm sure I'd have levitated had he not been holding me firmly.

I don't know how long we lay there together. There was no sense of time in my altered state. All that existed was the combination of Jesse's body and mine, and we were so deeply joined as to be one beast. I'd have happily agreed to exist in that state for the next decade or so. But it doesn't work that way, of course. I became aware of Jesse's breathing, as it grew deeper. The change jarred me out of my meditation, and I knew he was about to gift me again.

"Fuck me Jesus!" Jesse shouted as he erupted deep inside me. I felt each spasm. I welcomed the flow of Jesse's deepest self as it entered the recesses of mine. When he had recovered a bit, he said, "I want to see my boy's pretty dick." I lifted my body and sat back down on Jesse's dozen inches, which still filled me totally. "I want boy juice on my chest. Give it to your daddy. Give me what I want." I think it took maybe three or four strokes. I shot farther than usual. I even hit Jesse's beard with one spurt. That made him laugh. It made me laugh, too.

We shared big, cummy kisses and more laughter. Eventually, it was time for me to surrender the part of Jesse I held captive. I was reluctant to do so. Its entry had been so difficult, and yet, once in, it felt as natural as if it had always been mine. "My God, Justin," Jesse said. "if you were my boy it might kill me. I wouldn't be able to keep my hands off you. I wouldn't be willing to let you out of my sight or out of my bed, except for meals and maybe a shower once a week or so."

"I think I could get used to that. Let's talk. Thank you, Jesse, for the hospitality. The sex was amazing. Truly. And you even made breakfast. You're not at all what I bargained for. You're so much more. I have to leave. I do have to work tonight. You'll hear from me."

"Good," Jesse said. "Justin, I meant what I said. I could get serious. Or I could be a playmate. Your call."

"I don't know, Jesse. I have a lot to think about. I told you I have—had—a boyfriend. I love him so much. I'm still in shock."

"What happened?"

"I fucked up, Jesse. I can't talk about it. And I wouldn't be proud of coming *here* while there's still a chance I could get him back, except that you're such a quality guy. I'll never regret our time together. Gotta go." Jesse kissed me and then sent me on my way. I put the previous hours out of my mind, mostly, as I got myself home, showered, and dressed for the restaurant. Working next to Cole all evening would be interesting, no doubt. But I'd lived through worse, hadn't I?

Chapter Ten

Meeting Maggie for breakfast on Friday was a rare treat for me. We hadn't gotten together outside of work in the last year, probably. After all our meals and drinks together and our shared hopes and dreams—in Providence, the previous decade—our New York lives had been rather more separate. When Maggie suggested Sarabeth's—the big one on Park Avenue South—I was happy to agree. It's not my favorite vibe, but I knew there would be satisfying American breakfast fare from another era—or, more likely, from an era we imagine existed.

"Justin, I'm so glad we could do this. I feel like I haven't really talked to you in ages, and I miss it."

"So do I, Maggie," I said. "What should I order?"

"Whatever your little heart desires," she said. "Some variation on Eggs Benedict is usually a safe bet."

"Choose one for me," I said. And she did—the one with smoked salmon. I was delighted to be with Maggie, on a quiet morning. It made me feel more settled, more normal than I had felt since Cole's departure. And the coffee was not bad. "Maggie, I've missed being with you, too," I said.

"Who'd have thought life could get so hectic?" she said. "I kept waiting for life to start, and now I'm in it up to my ass. I'm not complaining, mind you. I always wanted to be busy. But then I always wanted to have dear friends in my life. Like you. And it's not so easy to honor those friendships these days."

"Maggie, I think you're wrong," I said. "You honor me every day you're in my life—every day that you make your part of *Civitavecchia* work. Beautifully. And now I'm going to shut up. Unless you want to see a silly faggot in tears."

Maggie reached for my hand. "Do you want to talk about Cole?" she asked.

"Thanks, Maggs, but I think I'm talked out. Roger made me spill my guts, and now it's mostly about waiting, I think. I don't know what more I can do to make myself worthy of Cole."

"You've always been worthy of Cole, dear. Don't be so hard on yourself. So, let's talk about the future—our professional future, that is. We haven't talked about it in ages."

"Exactly," I said. "Roger and I touch on it occasionally. But I don't know. What are you thinking, Maggie?"

"I'm thinking we all have to be on the same page—the same calendar. I'm flexible. I'm restless enough to face a new challenge tomorrow, but I'm also proud of my work at the restaurant."

"As you should be."

"What I mean is, I'll stay as long as it's your kitchen and not a day longer." I took Maggie's hands in mine, and we sat quietly for a while. I didn't need to verbalize how deeply her loyalty touched me. She knew. We ate some breakfast. It was fine—a little cutesy, but satisfying. The waitress topped up our coffee cups. I half expected her to be wearing a little starched cap. We were in the middle of an Americana theme park, after all.

"I've been thinking, of course, about what I can bring to the project," Maggie said. "There are several different ways to go with this, but I think we should bake bread. Tons of it, if we can get enough ovens. Not only could we bake everything we need for the restaurants and the food pantry, but we could whole-sale it. That gives us not just cash but cachet. I can see especially millennials seeking out our loaves—they'll be distinctive, of course—because they're delicious, because they're trendy, and because they're baked for a good cause."

"That sounds wonderful, Maggs. I think it's spot-on," I said. "I'll tell Roger to budget in a huge bank of bread ovens. And you'll train bakers?"

"I'd love to, Justin. That may be more important than the bread itself. We talked years ago about a signature cake, something we can bake and ship all over the world—like *Sachertorte*. I still think that's a good idea. And I'd be happy to formulate it, if that's what we decide on. But it occurred to me recently that we can do something more dynamic. Remember the cronut?"

"Who doesn't?"

"Well, he's a great baker, but I'm better," Maggie said. "I can create a pastry that will have New York-ers lined up for blocks every morning. It would encourage people to come in for dinner. It would shine a light on what we're doing. And the press coverage alone could be priceless."

"*You're* priceless, Maggie," I said. "Let me speak to Roger about a meeting. It's time we all got to-gether." We finished our meal and headed our separate ways. Maggie went to the restaurant to start her day. So much of her work was daytime, and so much of mine was nighttime. I even got in a little nap before I dressed for work. My head was buzzing.

On Saturday night, we were especially busy when Roger came into the kitchen and found me dealing with an excess of pasta orders. "Sorry to bother you, Chef, but I need you to meet someone in the dining room. I think it's important." I would never doubt Roger's judgment of what's important.

"Just give me a minute," I said. I finished a pasta dish with a medley of shellfish and a sauce that contained a pinch of *peperoncino*, plenty of garlic and olive oil, and just enough tomato to give it a balancing sweetness. It was one of my favorites. Scotty had stayed late that day to help expedite dinner orders. I gave him the pasta plate and the three others we completed for that table. And then I went to get my starched coat.

I swept into the dining room looking as cool as I could manage. The restaurant was full. A contented buzz permeated the house. I hoped we could manage to keep it that way. I headed to the reception desk to find Roger. One of the hostesses—the cute little one with the short haircut and the hoop earrings—showed me where he was. I approached him. "Perfect timing, Justin. They're just finishing." Roger turned to his client and said. "Mr. Horofsky, please meet Chef Justin Alexander."

Horofsky rose to his feet to shake my hand. We did our how-do-you-dos, and then I insisted he reseat himself on the banquette. "Chef, I was so pleased when Roger told me he might be able to drag you from the kitchen long enough for us to meet. I had to tell you what a wonderful dinner we had tonight." His companion—a very handsome middle-aged woman, perfectly groomed and wearing a splendid emerald and diamond ring—nodded her agreement. "Every dish was perfect. I know these things are not easy to achieve, especially on such a busy night."

"You're so kind to appreciate what we do, Mr. Horofsky," I said. "And of course, we try to make it look effortless. You obviously understand the degree of organization it takes to pull it off."

"I've never experienced the pressures of a fine restaurant kitchen on a busy night, but I do understand high stakes and ventures that feel like a tightrope walk. Chef, please take my card," he said. "When you're ready, I hope you'll come to my office and talk to me."

"That's very gracious, Mr. Horofsky," I said.

"Call me Victor," he said. "I know a lot of people. I know people who want to make a lot of money, and I know people who want to do good in the world. And I think you'll know which kind you need to meet. When you're ready, Chef."

"Justin, please," I said.

"Give me a call, Justin, when it's time for you to move on."

"I will," I promised. We said our last thank-yous and goodbyes, and I headed back to the kitchen. By that point in the service, we had turned the corner from the threat of chaos to an easy, *controlled* chaos that signaled a good night. I looked at Cole and thought about how much I needed him—not just in my kitchen but in my bed, in my life, in my heart.

He knew I was staring at him, of course. He gave no reaction.

I headed for my office to finish up. Roger walked in. "Justin, do you know who Victor Horofsky is?"

"No, not really," I said.

"Well, he has more money than God. And he knows where the rest of it is. This was his first visit here. I think it went exceptionally well."

"Glad to hear it," I said. "He seemed pleased."

"Justin, I don't think you understand what Horofsky could do for you, for all of us."

"I'm listening, Roger," I said, "as I always do when you speak." I embraced him and gave him a chaste kiss. "It's about time to say good night to this night. Will you have a drink with me, after?"

"Of course," Roger said. "We don't have drinks together often. I miss that kind of face time with you. Our interactions in the restaurant are not the same. I miss your friendship, really."

I started to get a little misty. "In an hour or so?" I asked.

"I'll wait for you," Roger said, adding dramatically, "if it takes all night!"

"Don't you have work to do?" I joked. "I know I do."

"Aye, aye, Captain," Roger said, and he headed back to the dining room. When service was over and the kitchen had been put to bed, I locked up and found Roger waiting for me, as promised. We walked to our usual bar.

"Seeing Horofsky tonight made me think of the future," Roger said. "We haven't discussed that in ages."

"No. Maggie just said the same thing at breakfast yesterday," I said. "She has wonderful ideas, Roger. We need to get together."

"Do you have a timeline, Justin?"

"Good question," I said. "Before Cole came into my life, I thought I had maybe a year of this job left in me, tops. But then everything changed when Cole appeared. I felt so light and free that I wanted the arrangement to continue forever. Now, I don't know what I feel."

"Speaking of Cole, how's that going?" Roger asked.

"No change, unfortunately. Our relationship is strictly business. One night I was feeling such pain that when Cole looked at me, he winced slightly. Or so I thought. I could have imagined it."

"I think it's time to take action. Will you let me speak to him?" Roger asked.

"Jees, Roger, I don't know. I hate to see you mixed up in this. Do you really want to get involved?"

"Yes, if that's what it takes to restore your happiness. So, that's settled. I'll speak to Cole in the next few days. Monday evening is probably best. When you're not there. Leave it to me. I won't say anything stupid."

"No, Roger, I'm sure you won't."

"Meanwhile, I think we need to move forward. I think we need to take action while we're all still young and optimistic. I think you should call Horofsky within the next few weeks. As soon as you feel up to it. Asking for funding takes focus. And courage, of course, but you have plenty of that."

"I'm not so sure," I said. "But hearing your confidence makes me feel courageous. I agree, Roger.

Let's talk next week and build a detailed plan for the future. And get Maggie in on it. I wanted Cole with us, but not this way, Roger. I couldn't bear it." The combination of fatigue, alcohol, heartache, and guilt took me over. I started to cry.

Roger took my hand and squeezed it. He said, "You're not alone, Pookie. You've got me. And I'm every bit as fierce as you are. Let's take this one step at a time. First Cole, and then the world!" We both started to laugh. I took a few deep breaths and pulled myself together.

"Thanks, Roger. You're always the best medicine. Will you come home with me and sleep over tonight?"

"Oh, Justin, this is bad timing. I have a million things to do in the morning." Roger paused, and then he said, "But, yes. I'd like that."

"Good," I said. "Let's get home." And that's what we did. Welcoming Roger for only the second time in maybe four years was a warm pleasure. I was glad the bedsheets were reasonably clean, and that the rest of my apartment looked presentable. We had a nightcap. We brushed our teeth. And then we headed for bed.

As we stripped, I was aware that Roger's tight little body was just as hot as I remembered it. And I think he looked at me with considerable lust, as well. But that was not our purpose, that winter night. We were together to affirm our friendship. Our love. I'd have done anything Roger asked. And I suspect he'd have complied with any request of mine. But that was not it. No requests. No demands.

We got into bed and I pulled up the comforter. We reached for each other, in unison. We shared a long hug and a deep kiss. "I love you, Justin." Roger said.

"And I love you, Roger," I said. "Sleep well." Eventually, we relaxed our embrace, and Roger rolled over. I pulled his body to mine. I put my arm around him and held him close. My stiff dick was pressed against his glorious ass. There was stiffness on Roger's side, as well. I brushed against it as I settled into a comfortable embrace. The arrangement felt right, but I wasn't sure I could do it. I wasn't sure I could hold that beautiful man against my body, all night, without tasting him or entering him.

It was up to Roger, really. The slightest signal from him, and I'd have pounced. I was so close to the place I most wanted to spend the night. My dick ached for the warmth of Roger's interior. I wasn't exactly restless, but I wasn't sleeping, either. Eventually Roger said, softly, "Justin, I have to get some sleep, and you're so tense you're keeping me awake. I can sleep with a dick up my ass. Put it in, if you want. You can stay there, as long as you're still."

"Thank you," I said. And that's what I did. I entered Roger. He sighed, softly. I savored his warmth. I moved my arm so that I was gripping Roger's tummy, to hold him close to me. His very nice dick rested against my hand. I whispered, "I love you, Roger." He began to breathe rhythmically, and then to snore softly. I did as I was told: I was as still as I could be. And then I quickly joined Roger in Dreamland.

Chapter Eleven

Monday night Roger phoned to ask if he could stop by for a few minutes. Of course I said yes. He arrived within twenty minutes, and I poured Scotch for us both. "The first phase of Operation Reunion is accomplished," Roger said.

"You talked to Cole? Do tell," I said.

"Toward the end of service, I went to the kitchen to find him. One of the line cooks told me Cole was in your office. I decided that was the perfect place to confront him. He was seated at your desk, finishing up the evening paperwork. 'Sorry to bother you, Chef, but I'd like a word, if you have the time.'

"'Roger, please call me Cole,' he said. 'We don't need formalities here.'

"'No,' I said. 'Cole, I've been very worried about Justin—and about you—since the breakup. I adore both of you, and I'm convinced you belong together. Justin told me his version of what caused the split, but I haven't heard yours.'

"'Yes, well, I'm glad you realize that I'm hurting, too.' Cole said. He got so quiet I was afraid the conversation was over. But then he said, 'Roger, I thought I could trust Justin with my life—until the night he showed me his heart. I can't talk about it. It's too painful.'"

Roger said, "Well, you know me, Justin. I wasn't going to leave it there. So I said to him, 'Forgiveness is a wonderful thing, Cole. If the shoes were reversed, you'd want mercy, I think. Just so you know, Justin had to dig deep, but he found the offense. And I think he purged it. I think he's a different man today—except that he's still desperately in love with you.' I let that sink in for a moment, and then I said, 'Talk to him, Cole. Forgive him. Don't let this fester. Don't waste precious time you two could be sharing.'

"Cole looked moved. He looked thoughtful. And then he said, 'Thank you, Roger, for taking an interest in us. I heard every word you said. And I promise I'll work on it.' Cole rose and reached out his arms to me. He embraced me, and he kissed me, to my surprise! Honestly, Justin, if I could go home to that kiss every night, my whole life would be different."

"Roger, stop torturing me!" I said.

"Sorry, darling," he said. "But I think things are moving in the right direction. I've got to go. Thanks for the drink."

"Will you sleep over?"

"No, Justin, not tonight. I have to be up super early. Ask me again another time." And Roger was off. I sat back down and poured myself another splash of my favorite Scotch—the rich one with the caramel note in the finish. Roger seemed so optimistic, and yet I wasn't so sure. I played the video of Cole's exit over and over in my head. It made me shudder every time. Every replay made me weepy. Eventually, I gave up on the possibility of anything positive ahead and went to bed.

The next time I worked with Cole, the following evening, I looked for signs of a thaw. But there wasn't a trace of spring in Cole's demeanor. It was as if the famous groundhogs had gotten it wrong—as if winter might continue indefinitely. I did my work. I can always do that. I headed home. I poured a Scotch—for medicinal purposes, of course. And then I phoned Jesse. "May I come over?" I asked.

"Sure," he said. "Just give me maybe a half hour."

"Yes, thank you, Jesse. I'll be there." I was restless, I was eager, I was ashamed that even the *hope* of Cole's return was not enough to sustain me. I was not making great sense of my life. I paced my apartment for twenty minutes, and then I put on my jacket and headed out.

I pressed Jesse's call button. He buzzed me into his lobby. I waited for the elevator. When it arrived, a cute blond kid got out, stopped to look at me, and said, "He likes them young. Good luck!" And he was off into the night. It spooked me a little—knowing that Jesse had rearranged his night to accommodate me. But I soon put that out of my head.

"Thanks for letting me come over," I said, after he invited me in and kissed me sweetly. Jesse was exactly as I remembered him, only maybe not quite as massive as I had thought.

"I told you to call. I meant it," he said. "Something to drink?"

"Sure. Do you have any Scotch?" I asked.

"I do. How do you want it? The Scotch," Jesse said as he smiled broadly.

"One ice cube and a splash of water, please." Jesse made my drink and brought it to me. We sat in his living room. I sipped my Scotch. It was not my brand but still delicious. I looked at Jesse. He smiled patiently. Then I got up and walked to him. He rose and embraced me—quite tenderly. I let loose and started to cry a little. Just a few silent tears. Nothing much. Then I said, "Thank you, Jesse. I'm so desperately unhappy. I couldn't bear the thought of being alone tonight. And I didn't know where else to turn."

Jesse said, "Whoa, Justin, what's happening here? I told you I'm available for play. That's fine. I'll fuck you all night if that's what you need from me. But now you want my heart as well? I don't think so. I don't think I can give you my heart while yours belongs to another man. You're not stupid, Justin. You know better than that. Man up. Decide what you want. Justin, I adore you. I'll gladly participate in your life in any place I fit. This is not it. And if you can't figure it out, then don't call me again. It's that simple."

"Jesus!" I said. "You're way ahead of me, Jesse. I had no right to come here tonight."

"Don't be dramatic," he said. "If you want to fuck, then I'm ready. I'm always ready. But love, Justin? Something else entirely."

"I feel so childish," I said. "I don't really know why I thought I could ask you to fill my heart—without offering the same in return. Forgive me, Jesse. I won't call you again until I've figured things out. But I will call. I want to earn your friendship. Your love, really."

"That's fine, Justin," he said. "Why don't you finish your drink and head home? I don't think there's anything here tonight for the two of us to share." It was a chilling observation. But I couldn't deny the truth of it.

"Thank you, Jesse," I said as I headed to his front door. "Will you kiss me?"

"Of course," he said, and Jesse delivered one of his signature deep kisses. His beard against my face was like a thousand caresses. I was aroused, of course. I nearly asked Jesse to take me to bed. But I knew better than to trifle with that precious man. I said good night. And I left Jesse's apartment—reluctantly.

The walk home was just as miserable as the walk over. The wind picked up—as it seems to do at all hours these days. I rearranged my scarf and zipped up my jacket all the way. I was dressed warmly enough, but nothing could stop the cold that crept into my bones. In the ten minutes it took me to walk home, my teeth began to chatter. I set my jaw and sprinted the last two blocks.

The heat was off for the night, but my apartment was still mercifully warm. I went straight to bed, as soon as I could have a pee and get my clothes off. I lay there in the dark feeling sorry for myself. But as my body temperature stabilized, I began to feel a bit more like myself. I even flirted with a trace of optimism: Surely the Universe planned to restore Cole to me. Surely it did—but at its own pace, of course. I slept.

Chapter Twelve

Two nights later, I felt so empty when I got home from work that I picked up my phone. "Don't do it!" I told myself as my finger hovered over the round black icon with the orangey mask. I tapped it. My, what a busy night on Grindr! The whole neighborhood seemed to be looking. "Men need sex," I told myself. "Don't beat up on me just because I'm weak and needy. And horny." Fat chance.

I had only swiped up to the second screen when I noticed an interesting young guy. Nice looking, slim. His profile said "versatile," so I assumed he'd want me to fuck him. I was okay with that. Yes, mindless fucking. Why not? Not only did I send this guy my profile, but I offered to host. He accepted immediately. I stowed my knife roll in a kitchen cabinet— along with my intellect—and I prepared for a big helping of carnal.

He arrived in about five minutes—I told you Grindr is into proximity. Never mind Mr. Right. Serve me Mr. Right Now. I had already called down to ask the night doorman to send him up. I answered the door. "Justin," I said, and extended my hand.

"Jeff," he said as he shook it.

"Come in," I said. "A glass of wine?" He hesitated, but then he accepted. I poured. I noted that Jeff was better looking than his profile picture. His hair was longish on top, and it fell in soft, auburn curls. Kind eyes. A generous mouth. I made a slight attempt at conversation. "Jeff, how old are you," I asked. "Not that it's any of my business."

"Twenty-three," He said. "Twenty-four in August."

"Good age," I said. "Enjoy it." I didn't tell him how desperately unhappy I had been at that age. It didn't seem fair. "Will you come to bed?" We took our wine and headed for the bedroom. Jeff was such a nice kid that I felt a wave of sweetness flow over me. I decided he needed some gentleness in his life. God knew I did. I undressed Jeff slowly and kissed him tenderly as often as possible. He was slim and boyish. Definitely not a gym rat. He smelled of hay after a late summer rain—or what I imagined that smell to be.

When I finished undressing both of us, I said, "Jeff, let's get into bed." We did, of course. I pulled up the comforter, maybe half way, so we would have a little warmth to protect us from winter. The apartment was toasty enough, but I didn't want to take any chances. I kissed him. Deeply. He kissed me back. Deeply. So far so good. I proceeded to give Jeff what we call in the restaurant business the soigné treatment. I carefully investigated his body and invested my total attention wherever I happened to be in his bodyscape.

When I was tonguing the pretty little auburn tufts in his armpits, I was rapt. When I nibbled his nipples, I was focused. When I worked my way down to the really serious equipment, I approached it all with the same respect. When I teased Jeff's dick with my mouth, he sighed sweetly. He let me play with his foreskin and then swallow him whole.

I don't want you to think that Jeff was a wispy little thing who wanted to be "done." He only let me explore him for so long before he jumped into the process. He took on *my* body with vigor. And I must say, if I had known how to suck cock like that at his age, my whole life might be different.

He took such pleasure in our union. That was it, really. That was what mesmerized me. Jeff seemed to want to be in my arms and nowhere else. Hmmm. Imagine that. We bounced around for a while—a very pleasant while—until we reached the point where both of us knew we were headed—I think. I threw Jeff's legs over his head and dove for the pretty space between his legs with the soft, auburn fuzz. When my tongue had savored the region, I got myself into position to enter him. It wasn't that Jeff seemed fragile, but that he seemed so—callow, I suppose. I said to him, "Whenever you're ready. I'm here. I don't want to rush you. I've got all night. *You* take *me*. I won't move. Until you want me to."

Jeff eased himself toward me, and within a minute I was all the way in. He knew exactly what he wanted, and he got it. Jeff took it like a man. He gripped my thighs and urged me on. To the extent that I was thinking at all, I was aware that I wanted to be a good lover. Jeff's pleasure was my only concern. I liked his sex face. It was a rapturous combination of wonder and surprise. Our eyes only left each other's when we kissed. I knew, of course, when he was getting close. I maintained the cadence and the depth that had brought Jeff to that point. And then he rewarded my care with an eruption of deep-down masculinity.

There's something wonderous about being inside a man when he experiences orgasm. There's nothing quite like feeling his every pulse from the epicenter; or like enhancing his pleasure by filling him up and giving his pelvis something to grip. I've been on both sides of that equation, and I can't say which side is better. When Jeff's interior was all stillness, I began to move again. Jeff reached for me and pulled my mouth to his. I was still kissing him when my body surrendered the gift I had prepared for Jeff. He received it eagerly.

A few minutes later, Jeff said, "Justin, that was unbelievable. I'm pretty much speechless."

"Well, Jeff, *I* believe it. I was here, and I wouldn't have missed it for anything." I expected Jeff to dress and head home. Instead, he went to the bathroom to pee and then returned to bed. We embraced. Quietly. And right away Jeff fell asleep. I tried to rouse him, to send him home. I had no plans for a sleepover. But Jeff was in such deep slumber that I couldn't seem to wake him. I could have shouted at him, or shaken him, of course. But he looked so sweet lying there beside me that I couldn't do it to him. Instead, I set a 9:00 alarm, pulled up the duvet, and turned out the lights.

I eased Jeff to me and spooned him. He had been snoring softly, but he responded to my touch and moved his body tightly against mine. Jeff's warmth made me feel human. He wasn't Cole, but he was a living, breathing man who fell asleep in my bed. In my arms. I caressed him. I kissed his neck and tousled his hair as if he were my pet. And then I drifted off.

📖

When the alarm jangled us awake, Jeff sat up and said, "What time is it? 9:00? Shit! I'm going to be late for work." Jeff had a quick pee and then dressed as quickly as he could. He looked sweet as he bumbled about trying to get himself together. I was sorry to see him pull on his shorts. I quite liked the ass I had inhabited the night before, and Jeff's hooded dick looked so charming in the morning sunlight that I'd have gladly taken it on for the second time.

"Why don't you take a personal day, Jeff? We could spend the morning together. You haven't even had coffee."

"Thanks, Justin. I'd like that very much. But I can't today. May I call you?"

"Yes, Jeff." We traded numbers. "Off you go." Jeff seemed both in a rush and reluctant to leave. He kissed me, and then he was out the door. "What's going on here?" I asked myself.

"Other than some good clean fun?" I wondered.

"Do you really believe that?" I asked myself.

"What else could it be?" I responded. I told myself no other man had been in my bed since I met Cole. But that was not true, of course. I remembered Roger's sleepover. What difference could it make? Clean sheets erase all of that. Once the pecker tracks are gone, what remains, really?

Jeff did call me. At lunchtime. I was just stepping into the shower, and I didn't answer. I didn't listen to his voicemail until I was heading to work. He said, "Justin, thanks for last night. You're an amazing man, and I'd like to see you again. As soon as possible. I'll bet you make terrific coffee. Please call me."

I might have decided not to call Jeff, of course. But, under the circumstances, it seemed likely that

I'd phone him soon. Probably as soon as I got home from work that night. What if I proposed a Saturday night sleepover, so we could enjoy Sunday breakfast together? What if Cole decided to return to me and walked in on us? He still had his key, didn't he? There was a lot to think about—so much that I let it go for a day. I kept Jeff waiting. No doubt he wondered if he'd ever hear from me.

When I did phone Jeff—the following night—he accepted my sleepover invitation. Eagerly, I'd say. "I'll bring something for breakfast," he said. It was all arranged: I'd phone him when I got home from the restaurant so he could walk right over. We'd head straight to bed and get some much-needed sleep. And then we'd have the morning to share. Brilliance or lunacy? I wasn't sure.

Chapter Thirteen

When Jeff arrived on Saturday night he was carrying sacks of goodies for our breakfast—smoked salmon from Russ & Daughters, bagels and cream cheese, a red onion and a few ripe plum tomatoes. Jeff even thought to bring capers and a lemon. "You don't look much like a New Yorker," I said. "But I guess looks can be deceiving."

"I've been here five years now. I feel like a New Yorker. Sometimes. Except when I meet someone who grew up in Brooklyn—or the Bronx, maybe. They're the real thing."

"Where was home?" I asked.

"Indiana," Jeff said. "I didn't like it very much. That's why I decided on NYU. It was a little scary, but I figured if I didn't give it a try, I might get stuck in Plainfield for the rest of my life. And here I am."

"And I'm glad you are," I said. "Let's put this food away." We stowed everything but the bagels in the fridge. I poured some wine. We headed for the bedroom. As we were stripping, I said, "I know I promised we'd go right to sleep, but I'm not certain I can keep that promise. Could I have a kiss?"

"Just one?" Jeff asked.

"You keep count," I said, and I headed for Jeff's mouth. He welcomed me. We kissed for a while—at which point we were both standing at full attention. I led him to my side of the bed and sat him down. Then I sank to my knees and buried my face in Jeff's crotch—a warm and delicious place to be. And I proceeded to take his wonderfully stiff dick into my mouth and down my throat. It was a good fit.

Jeff put his hands lightly on the sides of my head and seemed to caress me as he joined my rhythm. Nothing pushy; nothing herky-jerky from Jeff. He was too modest for that. Too gentle. Before long Jeff said, "You're going to make me come." I maintained my cadence. And, of course, within a minute or two he did let loose. I instantly became totally still. I was no longer an eager pilgrim but merely a vessel for the holy tool and the sacramental fluid.

When we had recovered a little, I said, "My God, Jeff! That was a meal. Have you been saving it up?" His blush answered my question. "Let's get some sleep."

"Wait, Justin. Won't you let me . . .?"

"Tomorrow," I said.

"That's not fair!" Jeff protested.

"*Life* isn't fair," I said. "But you'll thank me in the morning when you wake up feeling like a young god—as indeed you are." We settled into bed. I spooned Jeff, again, and this time he felt my kisses on his neck and my fingers through his hair. It all felt delightful to me. Jeff quivered with the same delight, I fancied. "One question," I said. "How come you have all that great foreskin?"

"I was a sickly baby. They weren't sure I'd live, that first week. So they didn't bother with circumcision. My parents didn't care. By then it was no longer mandatory, even in the Midwest. Maybe two-thirds of my schoolmates were cut, and the rest of us, un."

"I'm glad you're in the "un" camp. It gives me something extra to play with. Get some sleep, Jeff," I said. "I'm sorry I kept you up with a stupid question."

"I love your questions, Justin. In fact, I love *you*."

I was stunned, of course. I had no ready reply, but I felt I had to come up with something. "Could we save that for morning?" I asked. I needn't have bothered. Jeff had already dozed into sleep mode. I kissed his neck one more time and then joined him.

In the morning, I found an old nightshirt for Jeff to wear. I couldn't give him the silk robe—*Cole's* robe. That was reserved. I made coffee, and we laid out our perfect New York breakfast. We talked and ate and smiled. Jeff was delightful company. We shared some facts from our childhoods and our more recent lives. Nothing too heavy. Nothing too negative. Nothing that could spoil the lightness of our morning together.

"Well, Mr. Businessman," I said. "Wall Street, really?"

"Justin, I promise you it wasn't what I had in mind," Jeff said. "I always wanted to do good things. I wanted to help people. I was hospitalized a lot when I was a kid. You don't want to hear about it. Eventually, they figured out the problem and patched me up. But I worshiped the doctors and nurses and orderlies and anesthesiologists and everyone else in charge of my care. I decided—at age nine, probably—to devote my life to serving others.

"I don't know exactly why I thought a business degree would help. But, that's what I studied. And I was good at it. And then I needed a job so I could pay the rent—not to mention my student loan. And three years later, here I am." I reflected on how I had managed to reach *my* current situation. I didn't discuss it. Instead, I smiled and helped Jeff finish the last of the salmon. And then we both knew breakfast was over and my bed was waiting for our return.

I'm happiest making love in the morning. Daylight adds a welcome sense of reality to it. And that makes up for any lost nighttime mystery. For example, I had only given lip service to Jeff's balls during our first encounters. I wanted more. I knew his scrotum would be laced with delicate blue veining. I knew I could be content to spend an entire Sunday morning there, lazily marveling at the wonders of bioengineering.

Jeff's dick was the perfect plaything. Much more than a mouthful, but not scary. Friendly, really. The kind of toy one would want to play with for a lifetime. And all that foreskin! Well, never mind. Jeff indulged my indulgence for a while, but then he said, "Justin, please, I want to taste your body. Just lie still and give me a chance." I did as he asked. I lay in the middle of my bed, spread eagle, and gave Jeff unfettered access.

He used me well. Wherever his hands and his mouth went, he brought warmth and sweetness. He nibbled with care. He grazed far and wide. And then he settled in between my legs. Men can't help it. It's what we want, whether we're doing or we're being done. "Justin, you have the most beautiful dick I've ever seen," Jeff said. I blamed that on his youth, but I also accepted the compliment.

Jeff continued to honor my body—and I told you about his fellatio skills—until I let loose. And just as I did, I shouted, "I love you, Cole!" It seemed to come from nowhere. And yet, surely it came from a place of truth. Jeff sat up suddenly, spat my semen onto my chest, and then got up and started to dress. It seemed unbelievable that the pretty young man was dashing from my apartment for the second time that week. And yet he certainly was.

"I can explain," I said.

"Don't bother," Jeff said as he pulled on his jeans.

"I'll call you," I said.

"Don't bother," he said as he tucked in his shirt and grabbed his jacket.

I dashed to my apartment door and stood in front of it, resolutely, with cum and saliva flowing down my body. I hoped that Jeff was too gentle to wrench the moist naked man aside, as I might have done in a similar circumstance. Too *reasonable*, I think, is what Jeff was. He looked plenty fierce. I had to do some quick thinking.

I said, "Jeff, you don't deserve this. You're a beautiful soul. I really can explain. Maybe you don't want to hear my story today, but I want to tell it to you, and I want to tell you that I love you. The fact that I fell in love with another man first is an important part of the story, but it doesn't change what we've shared. I'm asking you to forgive me and to be a part of my life. I don't want to lose you."

Jeff looked thoughtful, hurt, maybe just a bit forgiving—around the edges. He said, "I don't know, Justin. I'm so weary of worthless men. I don't know what to think. But, you know, email me some time.

If you want. I'll read anything you write. But don't fuck with me, Justin!" I reached for Jeff, and then I realized he was dressed and I was still covered in our shared fluids. I backed off and said, "I don't suppose you'll have another coffee with me."

"No, Justin," he said. "But I will answer your email."

"Will you kiss me?" I asked. He did, but rather at arms' length. His kiss was still sweet. I moved aside enough to open the door.

Jeff flashed a smile as he left my apartment, and he said, "I want to hear your story, Justin, and it had better be good." And he was gone. I felt like such an idiot that I returned to my bed and fell to my knees, burying my face in my pillow—ass upward—for a few minutes. Then I got up and put the kitchen in order—I can always do that, after all, no matter what—and then I got into the shower.

On my way to work, I thought, *Fuck you, Cole! How can you do this to me? You know you're the only man I want, and yet there I was with a nice guy in my bed who deserves a proper man in his life. And I can't be that man. Because I'm your slave.* I shed a few bitter tears behind my sunglasses. And then I got on with my life.

Chapter Fourteen

The following week, I phoned Jesse one night after work. "Thanks for taking my call," I said.

"Don't be stupid, Justin," he said. "I'm always happy to talk to you."

"I'm calling to see if you'll come in for dinner some night soon. On me. I want you to see my life in action. I meant it when I said I want to build a friendship with you. I want you in my life, Jesse. I'm not certain what that looks like, but I want to try."

"Thanks, Justin," he said. "I'd love to come. What's your slowest night—so I don't take up valuable space?"

"The only thing valuable is *you*, Jesse," I said, "but come on Tuesday. That's the night I'll probably have the most time to spend with you. Do you want to bring somebody?"

"No thanks, Justin. I'm happy to dine alone. I've gotten very good at it."

"Tuesday, then?" I asked. "At 7:00?" Jesse agreed, and I was feeling rather adult by the time we ended our call. It was a good feeling. I hadn't experienced it much, outside of work, that is. I plumped up a few pillows, turned on the bedroom TV, and settled in to watch some CNN. Even the day's news couldn't dampen my spirits. At a reasonable hour, I turned out everything and settled into sleep.

You've probably heard of the actors' nightmare—where they find themselves about to go on stage without a clue what play they're in. Well, there's the chefs' nightmare, too. It takes different forms but usually includes wading through various obstacles just to get to the restaurant—late, most likely. And then everything that can go wrong does. Not so different from an average night in the kitchen, really. But terrifying, nonetheless.

When I woke with a start, I sat bolt upright and tried to get my bearings. I suspected I had been shouting, considering the turns my dream took: I had just been dressing down a difficult customer with a full-throated verbal attack. There in the dark, with no one to comfort me, I comforted myself. I smiled as I realized it was only a dream. I assured myself I'd had quite enough of that for one night. I slept.

📖

I had told Roger to expect Jesse, of course. When Roger came into the kitchen to tell me Jesse had arrived and been seated, he rolled his eyes and said, quietly, "Where'd you find *him*?"

"Never mind, Roger," I said. "Please tell my guest I'll be right out to greet him. Who's his server?"

"Nancy."

"Good. Please tell her I'm going to order, and I get the check. Oh, and Roger, could you ask Alicia to make something nice for him—not too weird?" Roger saluted me and headed to the bar. I finished a few things in the kitchen and made my transformation to Dining Room Chef. Jesse looked just as hot in real clothes as he did at home in none at all. His smile was radiant. His handshake was warm and reassuring. I marveled, yet again, at what a glorious creature he was. "May I feed you?" I asked.

"Of course, Chef," Jesse said. "I place my life in your capable hands."

"That's a lot of responsibility," I said. "I'll try to rise to the occasion."

"You always have before," he said.

"Yes, well, you're about to see another side of me. Any allergies?"

"Not a one."

"Good," I said. "How's the cocktail?"

"Delicious. But I have no idea what's in it."

"That's probably for the best," I said. "Alicia does have flights of fancy. I'm going to start some food for you. Jesse, I'm delighted you're here."

"Thanks, Chef."

I found Nancy at the nearest POS station and asked her to put in for an appetizer *porchetta* and a glass of Frascati to start. "Please see me for the rest of the order," I said. "I know you won't rush him, Nancy. But let's give him the full soigné treatment." She understood, of course. I started to relax a little. When I got back to the kitchen, I ordered a little anchovy *crostino*—which was ready in a few minutes—and I instructed the next runner I saw to take it to table 17. I also made a mental note to ask Talbot how he felt about starting every table with a little *amuse-bouche*. We didn't do it regularly, but I thought it a good idea.

I asked Cole to scale down the seared wild striped bass special to make a starter portion. Nothing unusual there. Cole was flexible, of course. I had already thought about what I wanted to serve Jesse as a main course. I decided on the veal scallop with *porcini*. Light, but perfectly satisfying, with its veggies and little diamond of *polenta*. And since Cole would prepare it, it would be perfect. With a glass of Barolo. Salad with a little portion of *gorgonzola*. Maggie's chocolate-hazelnut dessert. Yes, it would be fine.

We had a surge in business around 8:00, as usual. I didn't have an opportunity to check on Jesse until after 9:00. But I was confident that Nancy was taking good care of him—with the expert help of Roger and Alicia, of course. Roger most of all. I had seen him with stars in his eyes before. And why not, really? Why shouldn't Roger and Jesse meet? I felt stupid that I hadn't thought of it before— before Roger walked into the kitchen to tell me Jesse had arrived. I had work to do, after all, so I put it out of my mind. Mostly.

When I could finally take a breather, I changed coats—and modes of behavior—and headed for the dining room. It was purring along, thanks to Roger, of course. Jesse grinned like the Cheshire Cat when I approached his table. He said, "Chef, if I ate this well every day I'd be . . . I don't know . . . incapacitated, I think. I'd have no appetite for anything else."

"Well, we can't have that," I said. "I want you back on your usual diet. I couldn't bear to think of you *not* making some man very happy. Speaking of which, what do you think of Roger?"

"I think his ass is probably even hotter than yours. If that's possible. I want to ask him over to my apartment. But only with your blessing."

"Give me a moment," I said. I looked around the dining room and spied Roger at the host's stand. I approached him and said, "*Monsieur le Maître d'Hô-tel*, you have a guest in need of your personal touch."

"*Oui, Chef.*" Roger looked a bit quizzical, but he left the task at hand with a hostess and followed me. I led him to Table 17. "Was your dinner satisfactory, sir?" Roger asked.

"Yes, quite," Jesse said. "As a matter of fact . . ."

I interrupted by saying, "Bless you, my children. Please excuse me." And I headed back to the kitchen. I felt a great surge of pleasure—and pride—that I had managed to do the right thing. Of course Roger and Jesse would be perfect together. And, of course, I realized, if I had fallen in love with Jesse—a little—it was because he was so lovable and not because he was *the* man for me.

When Roger brought Jesse into the kitchen, as part of his restaurant tour, I was a little nervous. Surely Roger told him about Cole. When Roger in-troduced them—my once-and-future, I hoped, and my never-was—I thought, *Well, fuck it! I'll have to tell Cole about Jesse anyway. I hope. Soon.* Roger was good at giving me the fish-eye when no one else could see it. I said to Jesse, "Please have a coffee at the bar, and I'll be out in a few minutes to say good night." And I said to Roger, confidentially, "Ask Nancy to forward the check to Alicia." He was way ahead of me. They left the kitchen. I stole a glance at Cole. He was every bit as stonily professional as always.

"I like having you here," I said to Jesse when I got to the bar. "You dressed up the dining room, and you make the bar look really inviting." Alicia stopped by to schmooze a little. I suggested a Sambuca. Jesse declined. I said to Alicia, "Please give Mr.

Randolph a little splash of *Vecchia Romagna*. From my bottle."

"Chef always knows best," she said.

I said, "Jesse, see how they pamper me here?"

"You deserve pampering, Chef," Jesse said. "All you can get."

Alicia said, "As long as he continues to attract a classy clientele, we'll gladly grovel." She poured a little brandy for each of us, and then she headed off to attend to her real bar business.

"So you really enjoyed your dinner?" I asked.

"I loved it," Jesse said. "And I loved getting to know you. Every moment, every bite taught me who you are. I also loved getting all the way up your ass, but this was even better. What are you going to do about Cole?"

"Jesus, Jesse!" I said. "You certainly know how to get to the point."

"Look, Justin," he said, "you're too smart to let this drag on any longer. He's quite beautiful, by the way. And I'm guessing his heart is even more beautiful than his face is. I haven't seen his body, but I can imagine. Roger says he worships you. What's wrong with this picture?"

"I can't get away with anything, can I?" I said. "Look, Jesse, I don't know how to get him back. I'd walk over hot coals for him. That didn't sound quite right, but you know what I mean."

"I do, actually," Jesse said. "We'll talk about this again. Can I call you?"

"I'd be honored."

"I'm heading home," Jesse said. "Thanks for a lovely evening, Justin. And thanks for introducing me to Roger." As we said good night, I spied Alicia just behind Jesse fanning herself dramatically in a gesture I had learned to read as "What a hottie!" I certainly couldn't argue with that.

"Alicia," I said. "Could I have my check, please?"

"Chef can have whatever he wants, and it looks like he has excellent taste in wants. I'm just saying."

"My, what a clever staff we have here. I'm proud to be part of such a smart family," I said as I paid the check. I meant it, really. Alicia knew I did. She knew everything. Before I headed back to the kitchen, I found Nancy and asked, "Did 17 tip you?"

"Generously," she said.

"So we're good?"

"Absolutely."

"Thanks for taking good care of him, Nancy. I knew you would. When Roger told me it was your table, I knew it would go well. Thanks again." Nancy smiled and went back to her customers. Service was winding down. Smoothly. I headed to my office to finish up. Roger knocked politely on my door.

"Come," I said.

"My favorite word. Justin," Roger said, "Jesse wouldn't tell me how you two know each other."

"That's because he's a gentleman. Gentlemen don't kiss and tell."

"I knew it!" Roger said. "How was it?"

"You'll have to find that out for yourself, dear," I said. "And you shouldn't waste any time, I'm thinking."

"Did you set us up?" Roger asked.

"No, actually," I said. "I was too self-involved to realize I owed my best friend a chance to meet my—never mind. It's done. That's the important thing. And I hope you'll take it and run with it."

"I intend to," Roger said. "Have I told you recently how much I love you?

"No, but I have an excellent memory," I said. "We're good." Roger gave me a big kiss and then headed back to the dining room to close up. I headed back to the kitchen to do the same. Cole looked just about ready to leave. I walked up to his station and said, "Buy you a drink, Chef?"

"Thanks, but not tonight, Chef." I was crushed. Was that "not *tonight,*" or was it just "no." I couldn't tell. And I was too tired to parse Cole's reply with any degree of accuracy. When everything in the kitchen was spotless, I locked up and headed home to my other life—the one that was far from ordered and neat. I went to bed. And, maybe for the first time in my life, I cried myself to sleep.

Chapter Fifteen

I did finally write that email to Jeff. I don't remember everything I said. I can't find the text on my hard drive, so I can't print it here. This is what I wrote, mostly, I think:

Dear Jeff,

I've had time to think about you and about what we shared. Had I known we were headed toward something special, I'd have come clean to you early on, I'd like to believe. But I was so involved with my pain and my loss that I ignored the obvious.

You probably guessed that my heart belongs to another man. He left me, but I still have hopes of getting him back. That makes me either optimistic or crazy, I suppose. Take your pick. But I had to tell you that the hours you spent with me filled my heart with such sweetness that I almost believed I could be free of my past.

I won't ask you to forgive me for being a jerk, but I will ask you to consider being my friend. I don't have that many, and certainly very few of your quality. I'm hoping you'll take me on. And I'm hoping you'll let me tell you about a project I'm working on that might be a perfect place for your skills and dreams.

Sorry to be mysterious, but these things are always so aspirational before they're concrete. Please let me know if you will discuss it with me. And please let me know if you will dip into the considerable reserves of goodness in your heart and find a place for me there.

I do love you, Jeff.
Justin

When I had finally composed my message, I moused over the send button and hesitated for rather a long time before I committed to it. After a few little edits, I just said, "Fuck it!" and pulled the trigger. Jeff answered my email, as I hoped he would. His response was mostly, "Yes, and yes." And that was exactly the spur I needed to push me forward. I spoke to Roger that night after work. We made plans to meet at noon on Thursday.

I also texted Jeff and asked him to the restaurant some evening after work. He accepted my invitation. I asked Roger to seat him at one of the bar tables so we could keep sending him small plates until he cried "Uncle." And I knew Alicia would take good care of him. Plus, I wanted them all to meet. I sensed a professional chemistry. I do know how to build a team, after all.

At Starbucks, on Thursday, Roger said, "I used to think you were the finest man in my life, and then you introduced me to Jesse. And now I *know* you're the finest man in my life, because you led me to my future. You're so much more valuable than you think, dear. You're a precious commodity. Let's see how we can monetize you. Let's start with Horofsky. Are you willing to meet with him?"

"Yes, Roger," I said. "I'll call his office this afternoon. But only if you agree to come with me. I'm sure I don't know enough about the money to make sense. I can talk menus and nutrition for hours, but dollars? Not so much."

"Sure," Roger said. "Try for a Monday so you won't have to worry about getting to work afterward. And I'll get one of the hosts to cover for me if need be." I was glad Roger agreed to join me. I really don't have a keen money sense. I can spend wisely for the restaurant kitchen, and I can balance my checkbook (electronically, of course), but sums over a few thousand dollars seem like play money to me. Roger, on the other hand, can crunch the millions with precision and ease.

"Do you have a budget?" I asked.

"More or less. So much depends on the scope and the staffing."

"Please, Roger, go big," I said. "Don't ask me to cut corners on quality, and please don't settle for a space we'll outgrow in six months. We have to start with twice the square footage we think we need and then grow into it. Anything less will be demoralizing for all of us."

"Well, Chef, I like to see you in fighting mode," Roger said. "I think you'll be ready. I'll finalize a proposal for Horofsky and email it to you. And we'll take it from there." I felt lighter than I had felt since the last time Cole made love to me. It was enough to get me through the workday.

I did phone Horofsky's office and make an appointment for the following Monday afternoon. And then I took that nap Roger suggested. And then I prayed for Cole's return as I dressed for work.

When Roger walked into the kitchen to tell me Jeff had arrived, he asked, quietly, "Where did you find *this* one?"

"Yes, thank you," I said in full voice. "I'll be right out." I changed into my dining room drag and headed for the bar to greet Jeff. He managed to look exceptionally cute even in a suit and tie. "I'm so glad you're here," I said.

"So am I," Jeff said. I joined him at the little bar table. "You look very grand, Chef."

"Yes, well, don't let appearances fool you, Jeff. You know better. The last time you saw me I was not exactly starched and professional."

"No, but you looked so vulnerable and contrite that I thought seriously about staying for another coffee. *Very* seriously. But the whole situation was so ridiculous that I had to leave."

"You're right, of course," I said. "It's good of you to give me another chance. If you'll excuse me, I really should get back to the kitchen. Enjoy yourself! I'll check on you later." It was a busy dinner, but things went rather smoothly. The next time I checked on Jeff, he looked totally comfortable with the food I ordered and the drink Alicia arranged for him. Jeff also seemed to be enjoying the attentions of a gorgeous little bar server guy who was flirting very sweetly. I'm sure *I* must have been that young once, but I couldn't prove it.

"Did we pamper you?" I asked, when service was winding down and I could join Jeff for a few minutes.

"Justin, this is a wonderful place! I work with people who come here all the time, and yet I somehow never did. Thanks for correcting that."

"Can we tempt you with a tiny sweet?" I asked.

"I think you could tempt me with just about anything at this point, Chef."

"Good," I said, "and let Alicia know when you're ready for a coffee. Hers is even better than mine, if you can believe it."

"Justin," Jeff said quietly, "this has been a delightful evening. I've loved every bite, and I've loved seeing you again. But you have me a little off-balance. Again. What do you want from me, Justin?"

"An excellent question," I said. "As it happens, I want a great deal from you, Jeff. I want you to commit your talent and training and passion for doing good to the project that Roger and I are working on. Most of us really. Will you let me be mysterious for a while longer? I hesitate to ask you to trust me, but I will. And I'll ask you to be my friend."

"Interesting," Jeff said. "You seem to know so much about me, and yet I know almost nothing about you, except that you're handsome, you're a considerate lover, and you run a great kitchen. And now you're asking me for a commitment."

"I am."

"Did you get him back?"

"No, not yet."

"I'd like some clarity. I'm assuming we'll never make love again. Is that the reality? Just so I'll know."

"Jesus, Jeff," I said. "You're such a gentle man, and yet you can throw daggers at my heart. I meant it when I told you I love you. But Cole is my destiny. And if I can't have him beside me, then . . . Jeff. It's late. I'm tired. Maybe I'm not making a whole lot of sense. Could we talk again in a few days?"

"Of course, Chef," Jeff said indulgently. He also looked a little misty. I had never seen his liquid-blue eyes well up like that.

As I rose to leave, I extended my hand. Jeff stood and shook it warmly. "*Civitavecchia* is honored by your visit," I said.

"Thanks, Chef," Jeff said. "I look forward to hearing from you." I headed back to the kitchen to finish up. It would be an early night—if 11:30 is your idea of early. It was mine, in those days. When I returned to the bar to settle Jeff's check, Alicia said:

"My, Chef, you certainly have interesting taste in men—from the lily white to the black as night. Remind me to ask for your help the next time I'm husband-hunting."

"That would be an honor," I said. "But too difficult to find someone worthy of you. I know a few eligible straight men . . . sorry, I didn't ask if you like straight men."

"It depends on how well hung they are," Alicia said.

"Now we're getting to the meat of the issue. I'll file away your preferences for the future. Meanwhile, what did you think of Jeff? As a businessman, I mean."

Alicia was thoughtful. She said, "He seems sharp as a tack and kind-hearted at the same time. Good combination."

"I hoped you'd think so," I said. "Of course you know I want him for our team. I'll speak to Roger. We have to get together. It's been too long."

"Yes, Chef," Alicia said. "How about Cole?"

"Thanks for asking, Alicia, but don't. I'll text you with some possible times for all of us to get together." And then I headed for my office to finish up the day's paperwork. When Roger stopped by to say good night, I asked him, "What do you think of Jeff?"

"Personally, or professionally?" he asked.

"How about both?"

"He seems like a very nice man. I'll bet he's a generous lover. You don't have to share the details—unless you want to. Jeff's pretty, of course—in a puppy-doggish way. I can imagine men falling desperately in love with him." Roger gave me the eye. "But I smelled substance there, too. Spine. I think I could trust him, if need be."

"Good," I said. "Will you call me tomorrow? To set a date for a meeting?"

"With pleasure, my dear. Get some rest." That was my intention. I returned to the kitchen to finish up. I saw Cole closing down our station. Expertly, of course. Cole was—Cole. He was perfect. He was handsome, he was talented, and he loved me. I knew he did. I wouldn't have survived our breakup if I had thought Cole stopped loving me. *That* would have been the event that sent me to my collection of ultra-sharp blades for relief from my pain.

I clung to the idea of Cole's love for me as I headed home. Alone. My new normal. And off to bed. Alone.

Chapter Sixteen

Roger is such a good organizer. He managed to find a time—and a place—for some of us to get together for the first real planning meeting. Everything that came before had been two of us, or at most, three of us, saying, "Wouldn't it be great if we could all get together and solve the problem of hunger in New York City?" It was a weekday, so we couldn't assemble my entire Dream Team. That would have to wait—for a Sunday morning, maybe, in the not-too-distant future. I hoped.

But five of us were available to gather that Tuesday morning: Maggie and I from the kitchen brigade, Roger and Alicia from the front of the house and what would become our executive suite, and Liz from the pantry. I haven't told you much about Liz, except that she was an essential part of the *Civitavecchia* team. Liz had a genius for maintaining our provisions. And she almost made it look effortless. I knew better, of course. Once I watched her browbeat a delivery guy into leaving a 50-pound sack of onions that was destined for another restaurant—a competitor. She was just the sort of warrior we needed to run the food pantry.

Roger was glorious to watch when he was wearing his serious hat. He was *always* glorious to watch, of course—especially when he was wearing nothing at all. But his business side was equally impressive. "When I started work on a preliminary proposal," Roger said, when we had all been served our breakfasts, "I thought Justin and I were the only ones who'd really traded ideas about all of this. But of course that's not the truth. Maggie, for instance, has weighed in with terrific ideas for the role that baking can play, and I've included her thoughts. Alicia has been outspoken for years about the need for redistribution of wealth. Thank you, dear, for your full throat. And Liz knows better than any of us what families need to sustain their health.

"I've tried to include all of us in this little outline. If you want to read it now, that's great. It's not that easy for us all to meet these days. I hope that changes within the year. I'm hoping by then you'll all be sick of my face. Though I know I'll only learn to love yours even more."

"Save that for the investors, dear," I said. "Thank you for taking charge of this, Roger. Yes, let's see what we can share this morning. Roger sketched in roles for the five of us, plus Scott and Jenny, Jesse, and Jeff. That feels like The Team, to me." I didn't mention that I ached to have Cole with us. I couldn't go there. "So, let's talk. Let's see what everyone has to say this morning, and then Roger has suggested that we email him in the next few days with our additional thoughts."

While assembling five New Yorkers is like assembling five Israelis—at least ten different opinions—we came together rather quickly. Liz said, "Just talk to me about scope. And let me know where we'll be based. Nutrition needs don't change with the neighborhood. Tastes do. But even poor New Yorkers are relatively mobile. Get me enough funding, and I'll feed the whole fucking city. Roger, I don't quite see the size of the vision. I'm not complaining, I just don't know exactly where we are. If we can help a few hundred families put food on the table, that's good. If we can help a few hundred *thousand* families—even better. Think about it. I vote for more. I'll settle for less."

Alicia said, "Food insecurity is ripping society apart. I would never complain about the work I do with the secure. They deserve to enjoy their lives, too. But I think we're all here this morning because we want more. I agree with Liz. I think we need to aim high. There are plenty of billionaires in this city—several of whom we've all met—and there's no reason why we can't squeeze operating funds out of them. In fact, I pledge, here this morning, on my life, that I can guarantee the level of funding it will take to keep this project running."

Well, who among us didn't have a flair for the dramatic? And yet Alicia certainly made me feel like Mr. Wimp. Maggie said she was satisfied that Roger had characterized her baking ideas properly, and that she would be happy to move forward with whatever projects earned consensus. I spoke briefly about various dining strategies and ways that we could provide breakfasts and lunches, especially, for children. No one could argue with that, of course.

We didn't get to legal aid, day care, or sanctuary for abuse victims. We didn't have the leadership with us that morning. But I was confident that we did have those leaders on our team—as confident as I was about anything those days. On her way out, Maggie asked me, "What's up with Cole?"

"And I was having such a good morning," I said. "Oh, Maggs, I feel like I've done everything I can. With no result. I just don't know anymore."

"Well, dear, I don't have such a sterling record in matters of the heart, but I do think I can spot a match at twenty paces. And I always knew you two were right for each other. Liz said I should stay out of it. I'm sure she's right. But I'd like to help, if there's anything I can do."

"You always help," I said, "by being you. I couldn't ask for more than that. Let's see what we can do to help others. I think Roger is getting it right. What do you think?"

"I think you look tired, Justin," Maggie said. "I think you should get more sleep. And I also think Cole should take that corncob out of his ass and just accept that we're none of us perfect. I think . . . well, it doesn't really matter what I think, after all. Take care of yourself, Justin. You're precious to me."

Maggie pretty much stopped me in my tracks, as she had done before. Often. Through the years. I embraced her. I was out of words. She smiled warmly, as did Liz, and they were off. Alicia kissed me on her way out. I don't think she had ever done that before. It was a good kiss. Warm. Gentle, really. "Yes," she said. "I thought so. Your kiss is just what I imagined. Cole must be a fucking idiot to keep you dangling. I'm just saying. See you around the quad, Professor." And she was off.

"What's next?" I asked Roger.

"Feedback, really. I think I'll hear from everyone this week. And then we'll see. Justin, I think we're on our way. What do you think?"

"I think you're terrific, Roger. And I'm proud to be working with you," I said. Our table was already cleared, so Roger and I went to the bar and ordered mimosas. We sat, we sipped, we smiled. I said, "I thought the girls were terrific today. There's bound to be friction at some point. There always is. But I think everyone realizes it's not about them. It's not about us, Roger. Maybe that's why it feels so good."

"I love you, Pookie," Roger said. "I have to go. There's just enough time for you to get a little rest before you head to work."

"Yes, Doctor," I said. "How much am I paying for your advice?"

"It's priceless, my dear," Roger said. "Just follow it."

"*Oui, Monsieur le médecin,*" I said. "See you later." We parted. And I did head home for a quick nap before work. It was a good day. Wasn't it?

Chapter Seventeen

On Saturday night as I was leaving the restaurant, there was a loud scuffle in the alley. The thud of fists connecting with flesh and bone is a chilling sound. I dashed over to check it out, and there were two young skinheads beating up on Cole. I shouted, "Hey, back off!" No response. I always carry my knives, so I quickly grabbed the biggest one in my kit and called out, "Let go of him, or I'll put somebody's liver on tomorrow's menu."

They ignored me at first, until I lunged forward and slashed an arm, and then another, carefully, with a flourish. I always did have excellent knife skills. That got their attention. Their eyes glazed over like deer in the headlights, and then they ran off, to figure out how to stop the bleeding, no doubt. I reached for Cole, to steady him against the wall. "Let's get you to the hospital." I said.

"No, I don't think so," he said. "Let me catch my breath. Could we just stay here for a few minutes?"

"Of course," I said. "Take all the time you need." I stood there, holding Cole very carefully, for several minutes. He seemed to begin to normalize. I wiped the blood off my knife and put it away. I carefully refolded the handkerchief I used to clean the blade and put that away, too. You never know.

"I never pictured you fighting in an alley," Cole said.

"I never pictured you getting mugged. I'm worried you might have internal injuries. I still think we should go to the ER."

"No, I'm . . . I'm okay. Just a little fragile. I think I'd know if there were broken bones or anything."

"Well, there's no point in taking chances," I said. "I want to get you to NYU Hospital. I think they have the best ER. If you were spurting blood—like those boys are now—then Bellevue would have to do. But as it is, come with me." I headed, slowly, for the avenue to find us a cab. Cole was reasonably ambulatory. I hailed a taxi. I got Cole seated in the back, and then I ran around to the other side to join him. I asked the cabbie to drive carefully. He did.

Emergency rooms are always nightmarish, as far as I'm concerned. Even the good ones. They took Cole in for examination within twenty minutes or so. They also had a cop come to me and take my statement. I gave her all the particulars, and I suggested the restaurant itself might have surveillance camera footage of the incident. I also gave her my handkerchief, just in case a DNA match might help with the justice process. I suddenly worried that DNA information from my snot might cloud the issue. The police officer assured me that modern testing could differentiate. I gave her my card and asked her to come to the restaurant for dinner some time, on me. She seemed pleased. I began to feel a little less anxious.

Cole gave his statement, too, of course. And he promised to go to the precinct to swear out a formal complaint—within two days. The staff doctor released Cole after determining he had no concussion or other hidden damage. Two cracked ribs—for which there was really no treatment—would heal on their own, he said. I was relieved. "Well then, let me get you home. You've been sitting for a while. Can you walk enough for us to get you into a taxi?"

"Just."

"Good. Let's do it." I helped Cole walk to the avenue, where I hailed a cab and gave the driver my address. I asked him to drive as smoothly as possible because of my friend's injuries. Cole started to give *his* address, but I cut him off.

"Shut up, Cole. You're in no condition to be alone. I'm going to take you home, and I'm going to take care of you. Just relax. We'll be there in a few minutes." The streets are usually rather quiet at that hour of the morning. We made good time. I got Cole into the apartment and sat him down at the kitchen table. I made an ice pack to put on Cole's face. Two of them, actually. Marvelous things—bags of frozen peas.

We sat for a while. I poured some brandy. I watched Cole carefully, hoping to learn the real extent of his injuries. He seemed exactly as he claimed—as the staff doctor claimed—a little fragile but otherwise not in any danger. "I'll call Scott first thing in the morning," I said. "He'll cover for me tomorrow night. And one of his crew will cover for you. You don't need to think about anything."

Once I was satisfied that Cole was stable, I helped him to his feet and led him to my bedroom. We got his clothes off, carefully. As Cole eased into my bed, I pulled up the comforter and tried to get him settled for the night, as if I were tucking a child into bed. I sat beside him. I tried my very best not to, but I leaned forward and kissed him. He kissed me back. "I'm sorry for that," I said.

"I'm not," Cole said.

"Sleep, Coley," I said to him. "Sleep is the best medicine." And then I said to myself, "What a fucking day! So much for an early night." I got *myself* undressed, too, and then I gathered up all the bloody clothing and stuffed it into the hamper—to be sorted another day. I slipped into bed as carefully as possible, so as not to disturb Cole. My mind replayed scenes from the alley for a while. But after twenty minutes or so, I'd guess, the screen went dark. And I slipped into much-needed oblivion.

I left Cole still sleeping soundly when I got up in the morning and threw on a robe. First thing, I phoned Scott to tell him about the previous night and about the degree of support we'd need from him that day. He was gracious, as always. I promised to work on Monday to cover any shifts he had to rearrange. Then I started to cook some Irish oatmeal. Cole was still asleep. Good. I sat alone at my kitchen table—as I did most mornings those days. That quiet time—before the chatter and tumult of the day take over—is always precious to me. I can savor it all alone, if need be. Having Cole with me in the stillness of morning used to make it all the better. Could I maybe get that back? I made no assumptions.

When Cole ambled into the kitchen, gingerly, wearing an old T-shirt of mine I had laid out for him, I asked him, "How's the patient this morning?"

"Stiff," he said. "And not in a good way."

"You look better than expected," I said. "Much of the swelling in your face has gone down."

"I had expert nursing," he said. I served Cole coffee and oatmeal with a few berries and a splash of cream. I sat. The morning quiet returned. We shared it, just as we had done in happier days. When we had finished our breakfast, Cole broke the silence. "Thanks, Justin, for saving my life."

"You're being dramatic," I said. "Anyone would have jumped in to help you. Only I happen to be horribly in love with you, Cole, so that might have been a factor."

"Look, Justin, you know how I feel about you," Cole said. "And I think you understand why I left you. Roger said you did. What do *you* say?"

"I say *that* conversation is too intense for this morning. Let's focus on physical healing today. I arranged everything with Scotty. We don't need to think about *Civitavecchia* until tomorrow. I think a nap is in order. And then a little lunch. Another nap. Some movies. We'll order in something fun for dinner. And then we'll turn in early. You know, we've never had an entire day together like this. If only the cause of it were happy. Maybe tomorrow morning I'll be able to dig into the deepest remorse in my heart. But I can't do it now."

Cole took my hands in both of his. We sat for a while longer, and then he said, "You said a nap next? That sounds good. Shall we?" I helped Cole back to the bedroom and got him settled in. I joined him in bed. Cole rolled over and put his head on my chest. Then he winced in pain and said, "I can't do that." He rolled onto his back and said, "Justin, please get close to me. Your body is so warm. I need that."

I moved as close to Cole as I could without actually pressing any tender spots. I took his hand. We napped.

📖

When we woke, I asked, "Those assholes didn't hurt your dick, did they?"

"No, luckily," he said, "But I wasn't so sure about my balls. One of the guys gave me an uppercut to the crotch. Shooting stars before my eyes. Like that."

"And now?" I asked.

"Just a little tender. Nothing much."

"Cole, I want your dick in my mouth so badly I can hardly stand it," I said. "Will you let me? If I'm careful? A release might do you good."

"Justin, you don't have to sell me. Please, do it. I've missed it as much as you have, at least." I approached Cole as carefully as if he were some rare and fragile being—as indeed he was. I arranged myself between his legs and welcomed his precious dick into my mouth. I took the deep dive, only coming up for air when absolutely necessary—like a whale at sea, I thought. I let Cole's sweetness wash over me.

When Cole's body began to stir and his breathing began to change, I took extra care to be slow and gentle with him. I wanted it to creep up on him like a lovely surprise. I wanted him to offer me his deepest self, as he had done so freely in our first weeks together. But I wanted it to be a safe pleasure for his battered body. I wanted a lot. I got more than I dreamed possible when Cole took my hands in his and whispered, "I love you, Justin," as he surrendered the essence I craved.

I was greedy for it, like a man who's starving—as indeed I was. As soon as we were all stillness again, I started to weep. Cole said, "Don't cry, baby. I'm here." He took my face in his hands.

"Will you stay?" I asked. "I thought maybe I'd never taste you again. And now that I have, I don't want to live without you."

"Hush, baby," Cole said. "I'm not going anywhere. We've belonged together since the day we met. That won't change." I took a few deep breaths and got myself together—more or less. And then Cole asked, "What's for lunch?"

Chapter Eighteen

"You don't have to work today, Cole," I said as
I prepared our breakfast the next morning. "Scotty
can find coverage if you need more time." The previous day had been lovely and quiet—naps, meals,
embraces, lots of smiles. And a good night's sleep.
It was enough to remedy our typical chefs' sleep dep-
rivation. And almost enough to remedy my fears
about the future.

"I'm fine, Justin," Cole said. "I'm ready to get
back."

"All right, then," I said. "Dr. Alexander will write
a release for you. But only if you're certain." Cole
insisted he was. I got on with the business of breakfast. I had some kippers in the freezer, so I poached
two of them. Scrambled eggs, toast with jam and
good butter, hot milk for our coffee. The normalness
of our breakfast together was more nourishing for me
than the food. I'd have enjoyed it more without the
leaden feeling in the pit of my stomach brought on
by my promise to come clean—to open my heart for
inspection.

When there didn't seem much point in delaying
any longer, I poured us each another coffee and got
on with it. "I didn't understand, Cole, when you left
me. It wasn't until the next day that I found a little
clarity. I had to reason it out, to begin with. I

decided you're too smart to take offense at a comment unless the comment is offensive. So I had to dig deep. And I hated what I found. I had no idea it was there—the tinge of good old American racism. It was so subtle that it went unnoticed—by a white boy, of course.

"I did some housekeeping that Monday, Cole. I certainly used a lot of disinfectant. I found the stain, and I cleansed my heart, I think. I wanted to have a new love to offer you. One that's good enough. I wanted to prove myself worthy of *your* love. I did my best. The rest is up to you." That declaration took a lot out of me. I sat quietly and waited. I had found it difficult to look at Cole while I was speaking to him, so I had no idea, really, what to expect.

Cole seemed thoughtful. A good sign. And then he said, "Justin, I wasn't certain you could go there. But I'm glad you did. It's not for me to judge you. My job is to love you. And I do. More than ever." I leapt to my feet and grabbed Cole—too fiercely for his condition. I softened my grip, but not before I had danced us around my little kitchen and whooped loudly—like a kid who's been let out of doors after the rain.

Then I stopped suddenly and said, "Cole, will you move back in? I didn't ask. I want it so badly I jumped at the chance without getting clarification."

"Yes, Justin," he said. "I'll move back in as soon as possible—tonight, if we feel like gathering a few of my things."

"How about this morning? I asked. "Coley, you've made me the happiest man on Earth." And I was, of course. We straightened the kitchen and loaded the dishwasher. And then we sat back down at the table, held hands, and gazed into each other's eyes like lovesick teenagers—as indeed we were, more or less. "This feels like a good morning to talk about dreams," I said, "since you've made mine come true. How about yours?"

"Give me a minute to unpack it, Justin. It's rusty, I'm afraid."

"Take all the time you need, darling," I said.

"I've told you a lot about Georgia—Meemaw and Aunt Helen and my schoolteachers. But I didn't tell you about the Rev. Johnny. He came to town for a series of tent revival meetings and set up in the field behind our church. It was June. Right after high school graduation, so I had just turned eighteen. One night, after a particularly fiery sermon about the wages of sin, the Rev. invited me into his Winnebago and into his bed.

"Rev. Johnny was the hottest man I had ever seen. He made love to me with such passion that I was dazzled. It wasn't his first rodeo, I'm sure. I've often wondered how many men, women, and children came before me—or after me, for that matter. But he offered his complete attention when I was in his bed, which was three times, I think, before his traveling show moved on. I wasn't expecting something enduring. I knew it was only there and then.

"And I also wasn't expecting a take-away, but I got one. Our last time together, after Rev. Johnny had fucked me ecstatically, and before he patted my butt and sent me home, he said, 'Brother Cole, God has great plans for you. God wants you to feed his people. You can't escape His will, Brother Cole. He's everywhere. He was just inside you. And He's always with you. Listen to His gentle voice. Do what He commands. Be a vessel for His love, just as you have been a vessel for *my* love tonight.'

"I was weirded out, of course, and you notice I've never forgotten it," Cole said. "Within a short while, I decided Rev. Johnny had not only planted his seed but planted seeds for my future. And I still believe I have a mission to feed people. People who need nourishment. I'm happy to cook for rich people. But I don't think that's my future. I don't have a very well-developed God concept, but I do try to listen to the Universe. And it speaks, of course. It sent me you, for instance. This is getting creepy. I'm going to shut up."

"Don't you dare," I said as I took Cole's hands in mine. "You're making better sense than I ever can. But, as it happens, I think we're on the same path. I want you to read the little proposal Roger put together. It's just an outline, but I think you'll get the idea. I always wanted you to be part of it. But when you left me, I didn't think I could go there with you unless I had you beside me, totally. Is that what we have now, Cole?"

"Yes, Justin. If that's what you want."

"With all my heart," I said. "Cole, will you marry me?"

"Yes, Justin. I'd be honored to marry you."

I did another dance of joy—too athletic for the space and Cole's condition. "Okay," I said when I had calmed down a little. "We suddenly have a very busy day ahead of us. Let me give you Roger's proposal. And speaking of Roger, may I phone and tell him you're back? He'll be thrilled. He loves you almost as much as I do. Actually, he loves us *together* almost as much as I do. As does Maggie. As does Scott. And then we have to stop by your place for a few things—but not too many, because I intend to keep you naked as a jaybird whenever you're here with me. Should I shut up?"

"Yes, please," Cole said. "I can't get a kiss in edgewise." I did shut up—briefly, anyway. And Cole kissed me as sweetly as ever he had. And then our day took off like the roar of a jet engine.

Roger and I were both nervous about presenting Horofsky with the new document. It all felt so fateful, I suppose. So many futures riding on it. "Roger, I read your proposal," Horofsky said. "I think you can get a lot of support from City Hall and maybe Albany as well. They're always pleased when the private sector steps in to do things *they* should be doing. That's *moral* support, not financial.

"Still, noble causes that relieve government agencies of their responsibilities are relatively easy to fund. I'm confident I can get you open. One phone call to Bloomberg, for instance, and I can probably get you $15M in seed money. And then whatever else is needed. But after that, it's up to you."

"Thank you, Mr. Horofsky," Roger said.

"Victor," he said.

"Thanks, Victor. What's next?"

"Roger, you need to flesh out your proposal. Get a professional grant writer to help you. Foundations want details *ad nauseum.* Put in things that would even bore your mother. Play the game. And I'll help you win it. How soon do you think you can get that to me?"

"By the end of the month, Victor," Roger said. "Will that do?"

"Sounds good. Call me then."

"Victor," I said. It was the first time I had spoken his given name, and it felt odd. "May I ask a question?"

"Of course, Justin."

"Thanks, Victor. You said you could get us open. What did you mean?"

"An excellent question, Justin," Horofsky said. "I can find funding to get you to opening day, but projects like this require a staggering amount of cash to maintain them. If you don't have the perfect Director of Development, then *tebe pizdets*." Neither Roger nor I speak a word of Russian, but we both got the message. "And you'd better have the perfect Chief Financial Officer, too. Without total money clarity, you'll be shut down before the first year is up."

"I'm confident we have both of those team members," Roger said. "I'm hoping I can bring them to meet you, Victor."

"Good, Roger. Next time. Oh, and Justin—I sense you have another question." I smiled. "Maybe you're wondering what's in it for me." My smile widened. "Well, Justin," Horofsky said, "I like you two, and I like doing things for the public good. I don't get that many opportunities. But whatever I do, I always make money." This time it was Horofsky who grinned. "Write that proposal, Roger, then phone Maria and she'll schedule you for my next available timeslot."

Victor rose from his chair to signal the audience had ended. We shook hands. Roger and I thanked him for his time and his expertise. And Roger headed out of the office with me just behind him. As I reached the door, Horofsky called to me: "Justin, don't stop cooking. And don't check your ambition at the soup kitchen door. You may need it more than ever."

"I expect you're right, Victor," I said. "Thanks again." I smiled broadly and then slipped out of his office. Roger and I floated to the nearest Starbucks.

"What do you think?" Roger asked.

"I'm thinking if only Cole could have been there. If only he didn't look—and feel—like a mugging victim. Next time."

"Yes, and there's going to be a next time, Justin!" Roger said.

"Yes, and there's a lot to think about," I said. "Roger, don't lowball this thing. Write in twice the square footage you think we need. And twice the equipment. Otherwise we'll outgrow it the first year, and everyone will be demoralized. Be ambitious beyond your wildest dreams. That's the only way to approach this."

"My, my. I think I see fire in your eyes, young man," Roger said. "You were terrific with Horofsky, by the way. I think he has a crush on you."

"I doubt it, but I'd fuck him on the observation deck at the Empire State Building if that's what it took to get us off the ground. Roger, do you know a grant writer?"

"No, but I'll find one. Alicia knows everybody. She'll know who to get. Do you suppose she imagined Director of Development as her next job title?"

"Maybe," I said. "I doubt there's any title—even President of the United States—that she hasn't tried on. But maybe this will be challenge enough to hold her. I hope so. And if not? We'll deal with it. Gay boys can handle anything, after all."

"Damn straight! Pardon the expression," Roger said. "Justin, I'm heading to the restaurant, and I want you to go home and take a nap. You've earned it. And I'll send Cole home to you as soon as I can persuade him to leave the kitchen. He'll want to hear everything. Have I told you how thrilled I am that you and Cole are back together?"

"Yes, Roger, but it's still good to hear," I said. "I love you, Roger. Always did."

"Don't get me started, Mr. Hot Stuff," Roger said. "Let's get out of here." And that's what we did.

The evening seemed endless as I waited for Cole's return. My head was spinning with all the possibilities before us. Since the meeting with Horofsky, it all seemed so much more real. And with Cole back in my arms, it felt not only real but right. "Your little lover did good today," I told Cole when he finally got home.

"My little lover always does good," Cole said before giving me the kiss I craved.

"Let me pour you a glass of wine, darling. After you change, come sit with me and I'll bring you up to speed." And that's what we did. I was brimming with excitement as I shared my news with Cole. "I had a moment of clarity this evening, if you can believe it," I said. Cole smiled, indulgently. "It may seem minor to you, but it feels like a breakthrough to me. I think I know how to divide things up. I think I understand now how to balance the soup-kitchen-homeless-outreach part of our project with the nutrition for kids and with the fine dining."

"I'm all ears," Cole said.

"You're all *love*, darling," I said. "But never mind that. Here's what came to me today: Of course we've always planned to hire at-risk teens and the recently incarcerated. Well, some of them will want to learn cooking skills that will prepare them to work in the finest kitchens in the world. And I want you to run that training program—and that kitchen. Scotty and I will sort out the rest of it. What do you say, Coley?"

"I say you're crazy and I couldn't be more excited."

"Good," I said. "I want a hand in menu planning, and I'll do anything else you ask." To prove my sincerity, I dropped to my knees at Cole's feet and put my head in his lap. "Anything," I said.

"Does that offer extend to the bedroom?" Cole asked.

"It *begins* in the bedroom," I said. And that's where we headed.

<u>*Chapter Nineteen*</u>

It took time, of course. But Roger, with the help of an acquaintance of Alicia's, put together a proposal that was quite persuasive. Hell, after reading it, I myself would have invested if I had had any money. The language was graceful and quite readable, except for the sections that contained mind-numbing detail—as Horofsky requested. Before submitting the proposal to him, Roger and I decided it was time to assemble the troops—for the first time, really.

Sunday brunch seemed the mostly likely event that everyone could attend. Or a late breakfast, really. At 10:00. It worked. Cole and I got to the restaurant a little early, as did Roger and Jesse. The others arrived soon after. Jeff and Jesse had never met, so I took pleasure in introducing them. They greeted each other warmly, like natural friends. I was delighted.

But I was a little nervous as I looked around the table and realized I had been to bed with five of us— everyone but Liz and Alicia. I had told Cole about the others. There was no point in starting our new life with secrets. He took it well. We're not talking infidelity, here—only history and sometimes questionable choices. And, as promised, Cole didn't judge me. Neither Jesse nor Jeff had met Maggie or

Liz, so we took care of the introductions. Everyone already knew Alicia, of course.

Everyone made it to breakfast that Sunday morning except for Scott and Jenny, who were home preparing for the arrival of baby Justine. The future comes in various packaging, after all. For them, career stuff would have to wait a little while. And Roger's sister Rachel was still in LA. I don't think I told you much about her, except that they're close. Rachel is a skilled attorney, and when Roger asked her to join the team as our resident legal aid person, she jumped at the chance to do satisfying work and to have a good excuse to move back to New York. Rachel got her degree at Columbia Law, so she knew the city. And she would be able to get up to speed on local ordinances quickly.

"Justin and I are thrilled that we're all here today," Roger said. "This feels like real progress to me, as I hope it will to you. I put a proposal on every chair. I won't ask you to read it now. It's too early in the day for snoring." A polite titter. "But I will ask you to read it this week and to let me know if you're on the same page. Nothing is etched in stone, and I can fix a typo or rethink a whole section with the same ease. Let's get it right, this first step."

Roger raised his orange juice glass and said, "To Home!" We all repeated his toast and clinked various beverage glasses all around. New ventures are always exciting, of course. Most of the drama in life is in beginnings (and endings as well, but we won't go there). I couldn't help being buoyed by all the goodwill around the table. There would be clashes, of course. There always are. But we felt like such a united front that Sunday morning that I made a conscious decision to drop worry and enjoy the moment.

After breakfast we stood and milled around a bit, speaking to those who had been farthest from us at table and savoring the warmth of our union of hearts and minds. Jeff was the first to leave. "Well, you asked for a commitment," Jeff said as I walked him to the front door of the restaurant. "And here I am. It's like my decision to go to NYU instead of spending the rest of my life in Plainfield. I might have stayed on Wall Street forever if I hadn't met you."

"If I hadn't been such an asshole," I said.

"I like your asshole," Jeff said. "And I like you. Very much. In addition to loving you. Your heart is finer than you think, Justin. I don't take stupid risks for men who aren't worth it. Be very proud of yourself. I like Cole, by the way. More than I can say. If I *loved* him, I can imagine doing anything to get him back. I think I'm saying I respect your journey, Justin."

"Jeff, please don't make me cry so early in the day," I said. "Enjoy your day off, Jeff. Soon we won't know what that is," I reminded him. We embraced, Jeff kissed me sweetly, and he headed home. I watched him walking down the sidewalk with his hair glowing like burnished copper in the late morning sunlight, and I felt a great rush of warmth flow over me. Surely the Universe had blessed me richly with the quality of the lives that passed through mine—and sometimes paralleled mine. And surely it was pure evidence of grace. I headed back toward the table.

"Well, Chef," Alicia said, "we haven't had a real conversation in ages." She looked me up and down and said, "I like you in civvies. More than in whites. But I'm sure I'd like you even better in nothing at all." I'm sure I blushed. "But maybe that's going to have to wait for another life. When's the big day, Justin? I want to practice my toast to the happy grooms."

"Thank you, Alicia," I said. "I wish I had an answer. But everything seems so complicated these days. Wonderful, but complicated. I'll let you know. I think we need to get Home open first."

"Well, of course the timing is irrelevant as long as the two of you are together," Alicia said. "But I can recommend marriage. Wholeheartedly—more or less. You'll do a better job of it than I've done. That seems certain. Have I told you how much confidence I have in you and Roger?"

"No, but it's good to hear," I said.

"Well, I do. I'm not a stupid woman."

"No one ever accused you of that," I said.

"I don't stick my neck out for people I don't respect. I've watched both of you grow into fine, committed men. And I'm proud to be a part of your team." I embraced Alicia warmly, probably for the first time. When I released her, she looked a little emotional. Or maybe it was a trick of lighting. "Well, Chef," she said. "I'll see you at the store." She made her goodbyes all around and left the restaurant.

Maggie asked, "Walk us to the door, Chef?" I did, of course. "Liz and I were just saying how proud we are of your leadership. Roger could never have pulled this off on his own. He's a great organizer, but you, my dear, are the secret sauce." Maggie put her hand on my cheek in that gesture of hers that had warmed my heart for, what, a decade and a half? She looked into my eyes and asked, "When's the wedding?"

"Oh, Maggs," I said. "If only we could just do the deed and disappear into Honeymoon Land. But I think it has to wait. *We* think it has to wait until Home is off the ground. We'll see."

"Don't wait too long, Justin. Don't let life and commitments rob you of what you most want. But who am I to talk? I'll see you later." Maggie embraced me and then stepped through the doorway. Liz gave me a warm smile and a peck on the cheek, and the two of them headed down the street. Because Liz and Maggie left together, I began to wonder if they were maybe dating. It had never occurred to me that they might become partners. I had known for years that Maggie needed a good woman in her life, and while I had maybe assumed the same for Liz, it had never really dawned on me that the two of them might combine. I tried on the concept. I liked it. I loved it, actually. I made a mental note to talk to Maggie about it—kind of casual-like—that very evening.

Only the four of us remained. Cole went to the john, and Roger went to settle the check. Jesse said to me, "Justin, you're amazing when you're serious. If I weren't committed to Roger, I'd hit on you. Hard. But I am committed. And it's all because of you. How about a four-way? Cole is nearly as sexy as you are."

I laughed and said, "If anyone could inspire that, it would be you, Jesse. I won't rule it out, but I also won't organize it. You're on your own. Jesse, I don't think I've told you how pleased I am that you've joined us. Not just Roger, but Home. I've realized how safe you make me feel. Just as safe as when I was in your bed. Home won't work if it isn't a safe place. Without that, we won't be able to come to work with light hearts, and people in trouble won't come to us for help. And now I'll shut up." Jesse laughed and embraced me. We were still in that embrace when our partners returned.

"Don't mind us," Jesse said. "We're just planning our elopement. But only if you both agree to join us. Otherwise, the whole fuck's off."

Roger looked a bit startled. Cole said, "I'm in, but Justin and I only have a few private waking hours together as it is. I don't know how he'd feel about sharing that time. I know how *I'd* feel, but maybe Justin can give us some clarity."

I'm a lousy tennis player, but I know when the ball is in my court. "I feel blessed to have all of you in my life," I said, "and I feel *doubly* blessed that Cole has agreed to become my spouse. I'd like to try exclusivity, if he's willing. Cole, do you think you could agree to cleave only unto me?"

"It's a lot to ask," Cole said, "but I can stand it if you can." I grabbed him and kissed him as deeply as I dared in a public place. "Let's get you home," he said. "If we leave now there's still time for a short nap before work."

"Thank you, Coley," I said. "Give me a minute to finish up with Roger." Cole and Jesse headed for the door. *What beauties!* I thought. "My God, what a hot group, Roger. The body heat alone should be enough to get us to launch. I thought the meeting went well. What did you think?"

"I thought it was terrific. I'm stoked! I'm thinking we should be ready to see Horofsky in about two weeks. That gives everyone a little time to weigh in. Thanks for all your help, Pookie. I think we make a great team."

"No question. And thank *you*, Roger. You're a natural leader," I said. "You've led me astray more than once, of course, but now you're using your skills for the greater good. Kudos!" We embraced and then headed for the door to join our mates. I said to Jesse, "You'd better be good to him!" Jesse grinned. I turned to Cole, who looked delicious in the filtered daylight that flowed into the restaurant doorway. "Take me home," I said.

Chapter Twenty

Once the commitment was made, all around, the project seemed to take on a life of its own. Horofsky looked over Roger's proposal and suggested areas where the figures were unrealistically low. He also asked Roger to emphasize aspects of our mission that would be most appealing to donors and to de-emphasize the parts that were less glamorous. No major rewrites, just a tweak here and a tweak there. It took Roger only a week to polish the proposal.

The next time we saw Horofsky, he said, "I think I have some good news for you, boys. I think I've found the perfect venue. It's on the Lower East Side, in a neighborhood that still has a bit of Old New York left to it, as well as just enough gentrification to attract a good dinner crowd. It's big—an old factory building—and it's for sale. That's ideal, considering that the last thing you need is a landlord.

"And if you own the building, it will come off the property tax rolls immediately. One less financial headache. Roger, you filed for 501(c)(3) status, didn't you?" Roger assured Horofsky that the incorporation process was complete. "Good," Horofsky said. "Let's go look at it tomorrow morning. If you hate it, we'll find something else." _Just like that,_ I thought. But then, I had grown to expect that kind of can-do bravado from Victor.

The next morning, Roger and I headed—together—to the address Horofsky had given us. He arrived a few minutes later, accompanied by a real estate agent who looked rather bland and nondescript. But then most people looked rather bland and nondescript beside Victor. He made introductions. We all smiled politely, and then the agent turned the key—three of them actually—in the front door. It seemed to groan with the effort of opening after several years of disuse. It yielded.

The four of us walked into a space I had feared would be spooky, based on my assessment of the dark old brick exterior. And yet, it felt quite welcoming. Roger felt it, too. I was certain he did. It was big, as Victor had promised. The main space—inside the front door—had high ceilings and full-length windows that allowed in plenty of sunlight. Surely there would be even more light once the windows were cleaned. There was more than enough room for a retail space in the front and a large dining room behind it. Another floor above the main space would provide lots of opportunities for offices, sanctuary, and whatever projects we decided to embrace.

And that was the main space. To the left—through a central door—there was a second area, nearly as large. I imagined a huge kitchen. Perfect. And Maggie's bread bakery upstairs. The structure had supported heavy manufacturing equipment for nearly a century. Surely it could welcome enough ovens to bake bread for half the city. It even had a hoist system—which looked functional—for lifting in supplies and lowering down product to the street.

Yes. I looked at Roger. He looked at me. We shared an unspoken communication.

When our tour was over, we said goodbye to the real estate agent. The three of us headed to the nearest Starbucks. Yes, there *was* one nearby. Roger and I ordered our favorite coffees, and Victor ordered hot water. When we sat down, Victor took a sachet from his breast pocket and dropped it into the water. I took an interest. He offered me a taste. I settled for a whiff of the strong black tea he was about to savor—very Silk Road, I decided.

After we had settled and sipped for a few minutes, Victor said, "You boys are very quiet. What's the verdict?"

"It's more than I ever thought possible," I said. Roger concurred. "But *is* it possible?"

"Consider it done," Victor said, and he flashed the grin that I had found startling at first but that I had grown comfortable with in the time since. "I know an architect whose firm does all sorts of renovations, including kitchens and dining rooms. I wouldn't be surprised if they did *Civitavecchia*, actually, but I'm not sure. I'll talk to him this afternoon, if it's okay with you." It was more than okay with Roger and me, of course.

There was a great swirl of activity in the next few weeks that is now something of a blur to me. We were also working our full-time jobs, of course. But at the end of it we had bought a building, gutted it, and started in on the creation of a handsome, multi-function space that would be more welcoming than anything any of us had experienced before. I assumed Horofsky was taking a kickback from the realtor, the architect, and the various contractors. I hoped it was generous. He deserved it.

I couldn't tell you exactly how much money it took to "get us open," as Horofsky had described it. Less than $100M, surely. But maybe not *much* less. Victor secured it all. And it all came from legitimate philanthropic sources, as far as I know. We appointed Victor to the Board of Directors, of course. How could we not?

.....I dreaded the thought of having to tell Talbot about Home. I didn't fear him, exactly, but he was hardly warm and fuzzy. Our relationship through the years had always been cordial, but not exactly what you would call friendly. I suggested we meet for lunch at one of his other restaurants during a week I knew he would be in town. Talbot agreed.

We met at noon at his Asian theme park of a place on the West Side. Great food. And not *Civitavecchia*. He greeted me warmly. "Justin, it's always good to see you. You should try the wok-fried fish with the Sichuan sauce. The new chef refined it beautifully."

"I will, Jeremy," I said. "Thanks for agreeing to see me." We ordered wine and food. We smiled. We visited. We laughed about quirky little things that happen in restaurants. We touched on little issues in the kitchen I ran for him. It was all perfectly pleasant. It wasn't until the server cleared the luncheon plates and presented the coffee that things got quiet.

"So, Justin, what can I do for you?" Talbot asked.

"Yes, well, there's a project I've been interested in for years," I said. I was glad I had finished lunch, because I wouldn't have had any appetite at all had we taken up that conversation before the excellent fish was served and devoured. "Actually, *Roger* and I have talked about it for a long time. And now it looks as though it will happen." I described Home in as few words as possible. I wanted it to sound both noble and sensible. Perhaps it did. It did to me, anyway.

Talbot looked thoughtful. He said, "I envy you, Justin. I've reached a point in my life where I'm all in with big business. I like it. I like the money and the security. I like the prestige. I like being a little bit famous. And yet, I had dreams, too, once. I've achieved many of them. But not the ones you're pursuing. Go get 'em, Justin. Make the world a better place. We'll find someone to take over at *Civitavecchia*. And if they do *half* the job you've done these last years, then we'll be fortunate, indeed."

I thanked Talbot for his understanding, of course. And I experienced a degree of relief that at least the parting would be amicable. It helped to calm some of my fears about the leap of faith ahead—the one that would alter my career path irreversibly. "So, tell me, Justin, who are you taking with you—besides Roger?" he asked.

"Alicia," I said.

"I was afraid of that. And?"

"Liz." Talbot rolled his eyes.

"And?"

"Maggie,"

"Ouch!" Talbot said. "Are you planning to take the whole fucking crew?"

"Scotty, too," I said. No point in beating around the bush. "And Cole. And speaking of Cole, will you come to our wedding?"

"As long as it isn't in the next few weeks. As long as you give me some time, Justin, I'm sure I'll get over the urge to plunge a steak knife into your heart." Talbot was silent for a moment, and then he said, "Oh, Justin, I'm really delighted for you, and yes, it will be my honor to attend the wedding. And I insist you honeymoon at my resort in St. Kitt's. We'll deal with all of that. But, just so I know, when will you leave?"

"In about a month," I said. "I'll refine the timetable this week. I wanted to give you ample heads-up. Everyone has great respect for you and for *Civitavecchia*, so we plan to be entirely present right up until the last day. And we'll train our replacements as much as needed. You've always been so smart about staffing. I'm sure you have people from other restaurants you'll want to transfer. I can pledge we'll do everything possible to make the transition seamless."

"Thanks, Justin. Please keep me updated. I'm sure we'll make this work. But I'll miss you, Justin. I've always known how important you are to the business, but there's nothing like loss to remind us of what we've taken for granted. I wish you every happiness with the new venture and with the new merger. I've never had much success with marriage, but I envy those who do."

"As do I," I said. "I hope to be one of them. You've been so gracious, Jeremy. I'll always remember that."

"Well, I'm not feeling very gracious at the moment," Talbot said, "but I can imagine getting over that. In fact, I'll bet our paths cross in future. I know lots of people. I can imagine helping your new project. And I can imagine using your good name for some positive publicity for my brand. I don't burn bridges."

"Nor do I, Jeremy," I said. "Thanks for lunch. It was delicious. And now I have a kitchen to run."

I rose to leave. Talbot extended his hand and said, "Keep in touch, Justin." I promised I would, of course, and I headed across town to *Civitavecchia*. The heaviness in the pit of my stomach began to lighten. Surely it went well. Surely it *boded* well. Talbot bought our concept. Even a confirmed capitalist like him understood the need. Yes, we were doing the right thing. Surely. Yes?

The last month at *Civitavecchia* was bittersweet. It wasn't as if we were fleeing some odious servitude, after all. They had been good years. Only we all yearned for something finer, I think. Something to nourish the soul, maybe. I took comfort in knowing that Scott and Maggie and Liz—and Cole, of course— would be coming with me to our new life. And yet I sometimes felt extreme sadness at the thought of leaving all the others behind. You don't suppose I have issues with change, do you?

The last week was filled with little moments of emotion. The broiler guys gave me a beautiful scarf—hand-woven, no doubt, with the colors of the Mexican flag. I'll always cherish it. Little Luis came upstairs to offer me a slightly tearful hug and a bottle of Puerto Rican rum. The pasta team presented a box of pretty little egg tarts, baked by the best traditional Chinese cook in their family, they said. It was that kind of week. I got a robust handshake from Anna, the vegetable person whose career I had launched. And on my final day at *Civitavecchia* I was shocked to receive an embrace and well-wishes from the Salad Witch!

And then we left the structure and demands of a traditional food-service job for the surprises and self-discipline of the new and the unknown. Once I was committed to it, I was fine with the transition. Cole was more flexible than I. He simply moved forward and never looked back. I tried to follow his example.

Chapter Twenty-one

When the construction was nearly finished, and we had enough kitchen equipment—and volunteer staff—to handle an event, we decided on a Sunday open house. It would be a sort of soft opening for us, without the pressures of community need. That first Sunday, Home welcomed investors, politicians, city leaders, and everyone we could think to invite from the worlds of art and theater. The mayor and his wife attended. The governor and two of his daughters also arrived. We tried to buffer those two parties by keeping lots of other guests between them.

The Speaker of the City Council attended with his new husband. Leaders of various community outreach programs showed up, as did the Public Advocate and the Comptroller. We sent invitations to all the religious leaders we could locate. Most of them showed, including at least three bishops. It was a good crowd. It was an important crowd. The success of Home would depend largely on good will—and hard work, of course. It was cheering to see the former on parade that Sunday. As for the latter, Cole, Maggie, Scott, and Liz were making the kitchen work. The rest of us were pressing the flesh and trying to charm.

Alicia was in her glory. She looked stunning in a long Chinese silk sheath that fit her like a second skin. A slash of brilliant red lipstick with nail polish to match—jungle red, perhaps? Alicia had already met many of the guests, of course, and the ones who were new to her didn't stay that way for long. I had watched her work people before, at the bar. But even I was unprepared for Alicia's skill that Sunday afternoon, in our spiffy, spacious new home with sunlight bathing the room and the faces of New York's elite.

Alicia knew exactly which guests to handle herself—mostly men, plus the occasional lesbian—and which guests to hand off to Jeff—women and gay men, in particular. I was thrilled to see how smoothly Alicia and Jeff had bonded. They would, after all, be working together as closely as any of us would. Personality-wise they were quite the odd couple. But mutual respect is a formidable bridge.

Jeff seemed particularly good at charm—in a gentle way, of course. At one point I saw him talking with an older woman who had pledged an annual contribution that would do much to keep us in the black. A friend of mine said years ago, "You can always tell rich women. They may look as plain as an old shoe, but they always wear one piece of stunning jewelry." The dowager in Jeff's thrall was just such a woman. She was so taken with him that she became more and more physical, it seemed to me. I was afraid she might grab his ass, or something. But then I realized that whatever happened, Jeff would deal with it—just as he had dealt with me so elegantly in the past.

Jenny arrived in the middle of the afternoon with little Justine in her arms. Son Matthew bounded in ahead of them and attached himself to my right leg. "Hi, Uncle Justin," he said. "Do the bucking bronco." I tried my best to give Matty a good ride. I hadn't roughhoused with him in months, and in the interim, he had grown bigger and I had nearly forgotten how to play. When Matthew was ready to move on to the next distraction in the room—and there were many—I asked Jen if I could hold Justine.

"Of course, Justin," she said, and she carefully handed over her precious bundle. I knew that meeting my namesake would be a special moment, but I was unprepared for the surge of feelings that welled up in me as I bounced her—carefully—in my arms. I'm certain she smiled at me. I'd swear an oath to it. Justine gurgled sweetly and looked up at me with such trust that time seemed to stand still. "Justin, you're a natural," Jenny said. "Maybe it's time for you to consider having a child of your own."

"I'm going to leave that to you and Scotty, darling," I said. "I know when I'm outclassed." As I returned baby Justine to her mother, I said, "Jenny, you look so beautiful, I'm . . . I don't have words. Let me grab Matty and see if he'll ride on my shoulders for a while so you can go and see that handsome husband of yours. I'll bet he can spare a few minutes for his perfect mate and his perfect progeny. Tell him I said so." Jenny agreed. As she walked toward the kitchen, I couldn't help believing that Scott and Jenny and their babies were the perfect poster people for proper daycare.

I was still entertaining Matthew when Talbot showed up a few minutes later. I had hoped he would come. I asked Roger to look after Matty. Roger was more the "Let me show you the features of a perfect wine glass" kind of uncle, while I had been more of the "Wanna play horsey?" kind of uncle. I think children need both. Matthew seemed to agree. Talbot was warm and congratulatory. He greeted some friends and acquaintances. I got him a glass of bubbly. He was obviously skilled at working a crowd. No surprise there.

"Take me backstage, Justin," Talbot said after he was satisfied that he was properly visible to the assembled dignitaries. I gave him a tour of the kitchens and the bakery and the food pantry. He greeted everyone warmly. He said to me, "Justin, you've built a palace here! I can't even imagine a more ideal space. Cole can pump out beautiful dinners, and you and Scott will figure out the best ways to feed people who need it. Liz's pantry is so inviting I may show up there myself."

"Thanks, Jeremy," I said. "You've been so gracious about all of this."

"Bullshit," he said. "We both know what we're doing here, Justin. We both know it's about business and who we are and what our talents are and how we learn to live in our skins and sleep well at night. And, by the way, Maggie's bakery is stunning. Let me know as soon as you're organized. I want to order bread for the restaurants. I know it will be better than anything else I can buy." I was delighted, of course.

I loved seeing Rachel and Jesse interact. She had only been in town for a few weeks, but they were already family. I wanted Roger's happiness, of course, but I also wanted our legal aid person and our emergency services person to be tight-knit. And they were. Speaking of Roger's happiness, it was wonderful to watch him manage the reception. He focused entirely on our guests while at the same time knowing exactly how many glasses of champagne and how many beautiful little bites were offered.

The entire event was pure Roger. He could throw a party like no one else—and make it look as though he was having the best time of all. What impressed me most, and what probably made me fall in love with him (besides the perfection of his ass), was that Roger treated his staff like equals. So whether it was a Saturday night at *Civitavecchia* with the most professional servers in New York City or a popup event like ours with a ragtag crew of students and neighborhood recruits, Roger made everything happen without a moment of pique or condescension. It simply happened. And I prayed his skills would see us through many trials in the years to come.

Horofsky was beaming like a new father when he arrived that afternoon. I found a waiter and commandeered two glasses of bubbly. "Welcome to Home," I said as I handed glasses to Horofsky and his wife.

"I don't think you've properly met the missus, Justin."

"Bella," she said and smiled sweetly as she extended her hand.

"You honor us with your presence," I said as I shook her hand. And I meant it. "Victor found this building for us, of course. But then you know that."

"Victor thinks I'm not interested in his business, and most of the time he's right," she said. Victor smiled. "But this project brought out a warm quality in him that got my attention—paternal, dare I say it? Now I understand." Bella embraced me. "Where's this Roger I've been hearing about? Did I see him at the restaurant?" I looked around and found Roger nearby. I signaled to him, and he joined us as soon as he could politely leave the guests he was coddling. I made introductions.

Roger said, "We never did really meet, Mrs. Horofsky."

"Bella," she said. "Roger, I remember you from *Civitavecchia*, of course, but you're even handsomer in daylight. Do you think you could find me another glass of champagne?" I sensed they were off to a good start. I even wondered if they were maybe on the verge of becoming new best friends. Victor smiled and asked me for a tour.

"Of course," I said. "Come with me."

"What do you think, dear?" Horofsky asked his wife. "You've never been much interested in kitchens." She laughed easily and suggested he go on without her. The two of us headed for the kitchen door. "It looks like you got the whole fucking city to come out for your opening, Justin," he said. "Good for you! Didn't I tell you? If you don't hold onto these people, you'll be dead in the water."

"We're trying to stay focused on PR, Victor," I said. "We know it's just as important as mouths fed and lives saved. You met Alicia, didn't you?"

"Yes, I did," he said. "And I counted my fingers afterward. I could double my business if I had Alicia on staff. But I want to see her *here* as long as possible."

"That's generous, Victor," I said. "Come, see the main kitchen." I led him to Cole's new realm. We designed it to be maybe twice the size of a big New York City restaurant kitchen, so we could accommodate many students and many catering styles. The kitchen gleamed. It bustled. Liz brought in a tub of fresh herbs. Maggie gave the finishing touches to a tray of little *foie gras* things. Scott was focused on piping smoked fish mousse onto fluted zucchini rounds and garnishing each one with three salmon eggs and a tiny feather of dill. Cole looked up from his work and smiled. "Do you have a moment?" I asked.

"Of course," Cole said.

"Chef Cole Watkins, Victor Horofsky." They greeted each other warmly.

Victor said, "Great kitchen, Chef. I've never even boiled an egg, but I appreciate those who feed the rest of us. Maybe Justin told you I lent a helping hand."

"He told me a great deal more than that," Cole said. "I'm honored to meet you, Mr. Horofsky."

"Victor," he said. "I know you're busy. We've taken up enough of your time, Chef. Justin, does this kitchen go on forever?"

"No, but I hope our mission will. Let me show you *my* turf." I led Victor to the end of the room, where we had installed four huge steam kettles. "My soup kitchen," I said with pride.

"I never meant to disparage that, Justin," he said. "For my ancestors, a bowl of soup was often the difference between life and death. I get it. I like what you're doing. I like the fact that you want to get down to essentials. And I also hope you'll sell that soup out the front door to people who can pay for it, as well as feeding people in need. Monetize, Justin!"

I laughed and said, "You sound like Roger."

"Smart man, Roger," Victor said. "I'll confess it took me a minute to see it. I underestimated him at our first meeting. I thought he was probably just another New York restaurant host—a little light in the loafers. But by the end of our dinner, when he introduced you and me, I began to realize that both of you have substance. And that's really what matters to me. Fluffy people are like loose petals in the wind. No use to anyone. But Roger I like. Although I have to say I'd be scared to go to bed with him."

That caught me off guard. I didn't say anything about my history with Roger, of course, or about how certain I was that Roger had met his match in Jesse. I just pressed on with the tour. I steered Victor toward the stairs to the bakery. My office was on the way. I showed Horofsky how we had organized the departments. He said, "You know, Bella was very taken with you. She obviously has excellent taste in men. Speaking of which, Chef Cole loves you very much, I think."

I looked a bit startled, I'm sure. "He's my life partner, Victor," I said. "We've talked about marriage, but we've been too busy these last months to focus on it."

"Did you expect me to be shocked?" he asked. "I don't shock easy, in case you never noticed. And I don't judge. I like smart people. And I like attractive people. And you're both. I would expect you to have a quality partner. And now I know you do. Could I have a kiss, Justin?" Maybe Victor didn't shock easily, but I suppose I did.

"But why, Victor?" I asked.

"Because I'm used to getting what I want, and I always like to understand what I'm not going to get." Rather than trying to analyze the situation, I just accepted Victor's kiss, which was quite passionate, a little aggressive, but really very warm. He pressed his erection against mine. There was no mistaking it—on either side. And then he released me, flashed his Victor grin, and said, "Obviously Cole has excellent taste in kisses. I hope you two will always be very good to each other."

"That's our plan," I said. "And speaking of plans, there's much more for you to see."

"Could we save that for another day?" he asked.

"Of course," I said. "You're always welcome here, Victor. Home wouldn't exist without your help."

"I won't demand acts of gratitude—as much as I might want to—but I will return. And not just to buy a table at your fundraising galas. Justin, I have a warm feeling about Home—maybe even warmer than my feelings for you. I want to be a part of it."

"You *are* a part of it, Victor. A *founding* part of it. We all want you to be just as involved as you want to be."

"Good," he said. "I'm going to take off. Bella wants to go to some gallery in Soho. Or maybe it's Chelsea. Anyway, she likes to spend my money, and 1 like her to be happy. It's a good arrangement, I think."

"Sounds perfect to me," I said. "Victor, you're a remarkable man. Did I ever mention that?"

"No, but it's nice to hear. Go to work, Justin. Hungry people need you more than I do." We headed back to the reception. I felt a bit off balance, of course. We found Roger and Bella, who were enjoying a laugh—something about one of the clerics and his robes, Roger said. "Well, dear, shall we?" Horofsky asked his wife.

"Yes, Victor. I think we've had enough champagne for one Sunday afternoon. And I want to be sharp when we get to the gallery," Bella said.

"You're always sharp, my dear," Victor said. "Pity the gallerist who underestimates you."

"I'll take that as a compliment," she said.

"As it was intended. I signaled Val. He's probably out front already." We said our thank-yous and goodbyes. Victor kissed me on the cheek not twice but three times, in the Russian way. As did Bella. And then they were off.

"Holy shit!" I said to Roger. "He's a handful. What did you think of Bella?"

"She's a hoot," Roger said. "And I think she's a match for Victor."

"I'm sure you're right. Roger, is there anyone we were counting on who hasn't shown up yet?"

"Not really," Roger said. We've got politicians, civic leaders, clergy, rich people, all the usual suspects. I think it's a success."

"Thanks to you," I said. "Will you organize our wedding reception? I want to make sure it's lots of fun. Maybe we can have it here."

"I think that's a great idea. But I also have an idea for making it even better. How about a double ceremony?"

"You and Jesse? Roger, that's fabulous!" I said. "Would you really share the day with Cole and me?"

"It was Jesse's suggestion. But with so much going on, we haven't had a chance to really talk it through. Do you like the idea?"

"I love it," I said. "And I'm sure Cole will, too." Just then, two latecomers arrived—two young men who looked eerily familiar. "Excuse me, Roger. Let me greet our guests." As I walked closer to them, my smile began to fade as I realized where I had last seen them—in the harsh streetlight of an alley.

"You don't look so tough without a knife in your hand," one of them said to me.

"No, he just looks like an ordinary faggot," the other one said quietly. "We've been watching you. You didn't think we'd forget what you did to us, did you? Come along, faggot. We have plans for you."

The taller one pressed something hard against my ribs. I had never been menaced with a gun before, but I got the message quickly.

My first instinct was to stay put. Surely the boys wouldn't risk gunplay in a public space that still housed an elegant—though dwindling—crowd. The Police Commissioner might still be there, after all. He had been there earlier, for sure. The taller guy said, "Look, we'll give you a choice. We know where your nigger boyfriend is. So, come with us, or we'll cut his balls off." That made all the difference, of course. They hustled me out the front door. I didn't dare look back to see if anyone noticed my sudden departure. I was in a state of terror. I did exactly as I was told.

By the time the three of us had walked about a block from the building, I assumed I was a dead man. I lost all fear and began to feel nothing but deep sadness for poor Cole. That was my state when there was a sudden commotion and I heard a loud crack. I realized I was free of my escorts, so I turned to see Jesse as he cracked those two skinheads together for the second time. It was effective. They collapsed.

The next few minutes were like time on steroids. The police arrived and took the thugs away. I agreed to stop by the precinct to swear out a complaint. One officer assured me they were treating it as a hate crime. Jesse checked to make sure I wasn't hurt. And then we returned to the party. It was winding down, luckily. I was no longer feeling like much of a host. Roger looked slightly rattled, but he quickly regained his cool, and none of us said a word about the incident until every guest had left and the wait staff had whisked away all evidence of the party.

"Fuck!" Roger said. "Is that what we can expect from this neighborhood?"

"No, darling," I said. "Those were the assholes who beat up Cole. They wanted to settle a score after the bloodletting I gave them. It's nothing to do with the neighborhood. Nothing to do with Home."

Roger embraced me fiercely. "Just be careful," he said.

I got a little weepy when I gave Jesse a thank-you embrace. "My guardian angel," I said. "I thought that only happened in movies—knocking heads together."

"You'd be surprised," he said. "I know a few other effective moves."

"Good," I said. I could have elaborated on the effective moves of Jesse's that I already knew. But it wasn't the right time and place. I'd have been happy to let that be the end of it. But I had to tell Cole, of course. Everyone had to know. And then everyone had to get home for some well-earned rest. It had been an important day—imperfect, but important nonetheless. The first of many?

Chapter Twenty-two

When Cole got the phone call from his Aunt Helen in Georgia, I said to him, "Darling, you have to go. You have to say goodbye to your mother. You'll never forgive yourself if you don't do it. We'll open the restaurant when you get back. It doesn't matter when. Put that out of your mind." Cole seemed so _deeply_ sad. I had never seen him in such pain as when he had to confront the reality that the woman who bore him—and then abandoned him—was about to succumb to advanced breast cancer.

I meant it when I told Cole to forget about timelines. Life happens. What restaurant ever opened on schedule? Roger was supportive, as was everyone else at Home. I hated putting Cole into a taxi to the airport. I felt cheated, frankly. We hadn't slept apart for a single night since Cole moved back into my apartment. I knew the loneliness would be numbing for me. But I also felt a slight sense of relief that Cole would be spared some of the legal stress of the upcoming court case.

Rachel took Cole's statement before he left New York—written and notarized, and in video form as well. "Don't worry, Justin," she said. "The court understands urgent family business. The judge will not discount Cole's testimony simply because he can't deliver it in person." I found the trial grueling, and I was only just a witness. The thugs had eluded the police after they bashed Cole. I assumed they'd be apprehended in an ER after all the blood loss. Yet it didn't happen. But now they were in court to answer for that crime and for menacing me.

I did my bit. They were convicted on both counts. That, plus the string of hate crime convictions that preceded our complaints, was enough to earn the boys a good long stay "up the river." Decades. Did I feel safer as a result? Not entirely. Yet I had no choice but to accept my acquired sense of vigilance as the new normal. After the sentencing, Rachel took Jesse and me to lunch.

"So, men," Rachel asked over steaming bowls of Vietnamese *pho*, "when's this hitching going to happen? I'm not seeing much evidence of it." Jesse and I both laughed. She was right, of course. All of our marriage plans had been on hold since the day we closed on the purchase of the building. Everything personal seemed frozen.

"I'm a licensed marriage officiant, by the way. I'm just saying." We finished our soup. Rachel said, "Look, guys, I don't want to butt in, but where Roger's happiness is concerned, I'll take my chances. There's not much you can do with the restaurant with Cole in Georgia. Everything else is progressing smoothly, I think. My best legal advice is: 'Get married as soon as Cole gets back. Take three days to do something blissfully silly, and then come roaring back.' I'll send you my bill."

Jesse said, "Rachel, I think that's a perfect plan. I'll talk to Roger about it this afternoon. What do you think, Justin?"

"Brilliant," I said. "I'll text Cole right now. I think he'll be pleased."

"Good!" Rachel said. "I wish I could take you to get marriage licenses right now, but both parties have to appear. Jesse, you and Roger can do it any time. But you'll have to wait for Cole, Justin. It's not complicated. You just show up with ID and pay your $35." Yes. Joy began to blossom in my heart like desert flowers after a freak rainstorm. Yes.

Scott and I had a lot of decisions to make about how and when we'd be feeding children and their caregivers. And seniors, of course. And the homeless. Should we package grab-and-go meals? Should we be thinking about hot meals to add to Liz's pantry? Should we create another dining room or use the main room up until 3 or 4 in the afternoon? Scott and I spent more time together than we had since culinary school. I liked it. I think he did, too. It was a combination of dream-building and buddy-time.

One evening I asked Scott to stay on for a while and help me finish up a project. He phoned Jenny to tell her he'd be late. We ordered in a pizza and laughed at the incongruity. But there really weren't many food supplies in the house yet. Scott received the delivery, and I took some utensils to my office. I also opened a bottle of wine. *That* we had. The pizza was not bad. The wine was better. And the company was best of all. After our supper I took out my bottle of Scotch. That I had, too, of course. I poured.

Scott said to me, "I probably never told you this, Justin, but with Jenny's first pregnancy we talked long and hard about bringing a new life into this crazy world. We decided to let nature take its course, more or less. When Matthew was born—with plenty of fingers and toes and a cute little dick and two perfect little balls—we decided to make the most of it. We decided to do what we could to create a future for him. We never imagined, then, that we'd take that leap of faith again. But we did."

"Matty is perfect, of course," I said, "and I always get a little thrill when he calls me Uncle Justin. And Justine is . . . breathtaking. But really, Scotty, how did you two find the nerve to go there?"

"*I* didn't," Scott said. "Jenny's the one. I don't know how women do it. I doubt I'll ever understand their strength. They're just made better than we are, I think. You know, don't you?" Scott said. "You know what it's like to hold someone in your arms and know that you're home. Of course you do, Justin. I'm not making much sense. It's late, and I haven't had this much to drink since my bachelor days."

"I'll call Jenny immediately and take the blame," I said. "And I'll get you home. Come on, Daddy. The babies are waiting."

"I wouldn't tell you this, Justin," Scott said, "except that I've always felt I can tell you anything."

"And you can."

"Remember that time—those times—when we fell into bed together? Of course, you do. And you also know why." I was silent. "First of all, take a look at yourself, Justin. Who could resist you?"

"Millions of men that I know of," I said.

"Bullshit," Scott said. "You've never been turned down in your life, I'm guessing. Correct me if I'm wrong. But let's talk about Providence. Let's talk about you, and me, and Maggie—in various configurations. You do understand, I hope, why we all survived those wacky times and lived to fight another day." I was speechless. I poured Scott another splash of whiskey, even though I knew it was probably not a great idea.

"Justin, we love you," he said. "I haven't had a dick in my mouth since the last time we went to bed. Fifteen years ago? At least. I admire dick. I certainly admired yours. But taking another man's dick is not who I am. I took yours because I love you. Because I wanted to please you. Because I wanted to honor you. I'd do it again in a heartbeat." Scott stood and began to strip. I jumped to my feet and stopped him.

"Let's save the full monty for another time," I said. "Let me just grab my keys and we'll head out." I hustled Scott out of the building and into the first cab I could find. We arrived at his place in record time. I phoned Jenny rather than ringing the bell. She let us in. She looked a little stern but not agitated.

"Justin, I just made a pot of chamomile," she said. "Will you stay for a cup?"

"I'd like that," I said. Jenny quietly eased Scott into their bedroom and got him settled in for the night, I assumed. And then she returned to the living room with mugs of tea, as promised.

Jenny said, "Thanks for seeing Scott safely home. I knew you would." I studied the pale brew in my mug. I began to sober up—quickly. "Justin, we tied our boat to yours," she said. "With never a second thought. That's a given. We've never questioned what you and Roger put together. Matty adores his Uncle Justin, of course. And Justine will feel the same way as soon as she's old enough." I had no words.

"Scott is a good man," Jenny said. "He's a perfect husband and a perfect father. But please, Justin, don't fuck with him. Do I sound like a jealous wife? Maybe I am. I've always known how much he loves you. And don't think *I* don't love you, too. Because I do. But I won't let you . . . I won't let you be the Pied Piper. I won't let you enchant our family." I couldn't look at Jenny for a while. I sat. I sipped. I listened to a charming old mantle clock as it ticked away the seconds of my comeuppance.

Eventually I rose. I said, "It's late. Thanks for the tea, Jenny. Scotty is right, of course. He just told me tonight that women have all the strength. Especially his mate." Jenny smiled at me. Rather sweetly, I thought, under the circumstances. "I haven't always had boundaries around whose family is whose. With people I love. I don't have great history when it comes to family. But I'm willing to learn."

I nearly said, "Surely you don't have any questions about where your husband's heart lies." But I couldn't go there. I couldn't swear to Scott's devotion or my innocence. I couldn't find words of reassurance I was certain would be just right and not excessive. I looked at Jenny and tried to determine if she had a question for me. She seemed quietly assured, as always. I asked, "Will you kiss the babies for me in the morning?"

Jenny looked at me with the *What am I going to do with this naughty boy?* look that mothers and schoolteachers master early in their careers. She said to me, "Justin, I hope Cole has the patience to . . . well, of course he does. He loves you even more than we do. Go home!" Jenny embraced me, and I kissed her just as I would have done under any other circumstance. We were old friends, after all. And then I headed home.

Chapter Twenty-three

"Justin, do you have a minute?" Jeff asked me the next afternoon.

"Of course," I said. "I have all the time you want." I indicated the chair across from my desk. Jeff sat. I waited.

"Alicia wants to have my baby," he said. I'm sure I gasped. "That's not the whole truth. I'm pretty certain she wants to have *your* baby. But she doesn't think you're available. So she asked me. I'm willing. I've always wanted a child—I think. I just didn't know it." I stood, walked around the desk, and invited Jeff into my arms. He embraced me just as simply as he always had.

"Jeffrey, Jeffrey," I said as I resisted the urge to tousle his hair, "I don't know if I can get used to calling you Daddy. But I'll try. So, how are you going to do this?"

"The old-fashioned way," he said. "Alicia isn't willing to consider a turkey baster. And I support her totally in that. But I'm a little bit nervous about it. I've never been to bed with a woman."

"Yes, well, Jeff, you won't just be going to bed with a *woman*, you'll be going to bed with *Alicia*. And I can promise you she'll arrange the whole thing flawlessly. You'll like it, actually. You'll play your part with grace, as always. You'll plant the seed. You're a natural, Jeff. I've known that since the night I met you."

"Thanks for your support, Justin. I wanted you to be the first to know. But I wasn't certain how you'd take it," Jeff said.

"You imagined I'd start judging other people's choices? I have enough problems with my own. Tell you what, though—I want Rachel to draw up a pre-whatever agreement for you two. I can't see the point in going there without complete clarity. Will you let me ask her?"

"Thank you," Jeff said. "I hadn't quite gotten that far."

"Good," I said. "Rachel will be in this afternoon, and I know she'll get right on it. Jeff, you startle me at every turn. And I couldn't feel more honored to be your friend. If I had your heart I'd be—well, never mind what I'd be. The point is, no child on Earth could be more fortunate than yours. Really, Jeff. A baby. By you and Alicia." I started to laugh. So did Jeff. It was all so unlikely, and yet it made perfect sense.

"So, what are Alicia's terms?" I asked.

"Yes, well, she wants the child to be hers, but she won't deny me paternity."

"She'd better not!" I said. "You'll be providing world-class sperm. I can attest to that. So where does that leave you, Jeff? Will you be the doting dad or the occasional babysitter or the one who pays school fees or . . . ?"

"I don't know, Justin. I'm not there yet."

"Well, think about it. And trust Rachel to protect your rights." Jeff thanked me again and headed back to his office. I texted Alicia to ask for some face time. She replied that she had a luncheon meeting, but that she'd be back in her office after two.

☐

"Jeff told me about your plans," I said to Alicia that afternoon. "I don't know about this arrangement, Alicia. I adore Jeff, and I don't want to see him hurt. We understand each other, you and I. We're cut from the same cloth, in some ways. Jeff is different. He's nobody's fool, but he isn't—ruthless. I think that's it. I think you should marry him."

"My, Chef. How conventional!" she said. "What makes you think he'd even consider it?"

"Well, of course gay men are only interested in being wild and free. But I'll bet you could catch him at a weak moment. Alicia, you could do worse than having a partner who can give you beautiful babies and a stable home. And if he sucks dick on the side, so what? Who will *you* be boning? And who's going to change diapers when you need to go and testify before Congress on behalf of the homeless? I'm just saying."

"Well, that's a lot to think about," Alicia said. "Thanks for taking an interest, Chef. I'll get back to you."

"I was planning to ask Rachel to draw up an agreement for the two of you. Maybe it's a prenup. I don't know."

"I don't know either, Justin, but you're right. I'll talk to Rachel this afternoon. Smart lady."

"You bet," I said. I stood up to leave Alicia's office. She also rose and embraced me. Warmly. "I'm sure it will be fine. But, Alicia, don't you damage Jeff. Do it right or don't do it at all." She got my message. I was certain she did.

It was only a week and a half that Cole was away, but it felt like months. He was a bit shellshocked when he returned, of course. Big doses of family and life and death do that to us. "You need a few days to recover, darling," I said to him.

"What I need is more *you*, Justin," he said. "What I need is to get back into our lives. When can we get married? How about tomorrow?"

"Whoa, Cowboy!" I said. "We promised Roger and Jesse we'd do it together. Have you changed your mind?"

"No, Justin, but I don't want to waste time. I don't want us to squander our precious hours together."

"Let's stop and get a marriage license on our way to work tomorrow," I said. "How does that sound?"

"Lovely," Cole said. "And until then, will you hold me?" And that's what I did.

Victor phoned in the morning and asked, "Is everyone there?"

"More or less," I answered. "Why?"

"I want to stop by around noon. Bella and I want to stop by. We want to speak to you four boys."

"Of course, Victor," I said. "We always love to see you both." I was a bit puzzled. It wasn't like Victor to be mysterious. But I had plenty of other things to consider, so I got on with my morning. Maggie stopped by for the planning meeting that we had been talking about for a while. With Cole back in town, it was time to set an opening date for the restaurant.

"I don't know, Justin," she said. "I always thought the dessert list at Home should be more, well, *homey* than what I did for you and Talbot. I'm thinking sticky pudding and apple dumpling and pear charlotte. Are we on the same page?"

"When were we ever not?" I asked. "Just do it, Maggs. I know your choices will be perfect. And I know you'll consider the garnishing skills of the trainees. No more than six items on the list, I thought."

"Maybe five will be enough. Let me work on it."

"And the bread," I said. "Did Talbot come through with an order?"

"He did, actually," Maggie said. "Justin, it's amazing—the size of his empire. I had to be realistic about our production capabilities—right now. I asked Talbot to phase us in gradually. He was fine with that. I just formulated a dinner roll for him—harmless-looking but packed with flavor. I don't even know yet how many thousands of them we'll be baking a day. But it doesn't matter, Justin. We'll just bake."

"Maggie, we haven't really talked much since the breakfast that Roger organized. I don't know enough about your life anymore. Scott and I talk every day. But you're—somewhere else, most of the time. Will you let me in? I intended to ask you, after that breakfast, if you and Liz are building something, together. It certainly looked that way."

"Yes, well, it looked that way to me, too. But I don't think so, Justin. I don't think it's right. And I can't tell you exactly why I feel that way. But I do. And if I'm not all in, then I'm nowhere."

I sat at my desk, looking at Maggie, and my heart ached for all the happiness my old friend wasn't getting. "I wish I could wave a wand, darling," I said.

"No one's that big a fairy, dear. Not even you," Maggie said. "Besides, I love my life. I love my work. And I love you. Now, when's the wedding?"

"Soon, actually," I said. "I'll let you know."

"Give me a little heads-up, Justin. I'll bake the cake, of course."

"You'll do nothing of the sort, my dear. I won't have you working on my wedding day," I said. "But I will ask you to stand up for us. You and Scott."

"An honor, Justin. And in case I haven't mentioned it lately, I couldn't be happier for you and Cole." Maggie rose to leave my office, then stopped and put her hand on my cheek. "Yes, you'll be a great husband, Justin. I always knew you were prime husband material. I just couldn't have guessed for whom!"

"Oh, Maggs, I nearly forgot. Do you have any little cookies or something? We have guests—the Horofskys—stopping by at noon. Sorry to spring this on you, but I really should have something that looks like hospitality."

"No problem, Justin. I have some dough in the freezer I can easily bake off. Do you need more than a dozen or so?"

"Nope."

"Done." Maggie smiled and headed to her bakery.

I told Cole and Roger and Jesse about Victor's call, so everyone was ready to see the Horofskys when they arrived, right on time. We greeted them warmly, of course. There were lots of kisses and embraces all around. Roger had decided on a table in the—unfinished—dining room where we could all sit, and he and I served some strong black tea—not as exotic as Victor's, perhaps, but welcoming anyway. And Maggie's cookies, which were beautiful, of course.

"A harbor cruise," Victor said. "Yes. Bella and I will arrange the whole thing. The hungry have waited this long. They can wait another week. The four handsomest grooms in the City of New York need to be legally united before they have time to reconsider their folly."

"Oh, Victor, do shut up," Bella said. "We have a friend with a yacht that's big enough for maybe fifty guests."

"Don't worry," Victor said. "We'll serve soup for dinner." Bella gave him the evil eye.

"But it doesn't have to be dinner," Bella said. "If you'd prefer drinks and snacks, then maybe a hundred guests. It's your call. The marriage ceremony at sunset, I thought, just as we're passing the Statue of Liberty."

"Oh, the irony!" Victor said. Bella shot him that look. He retreated.

"I think you all deserve this," Bella said, "and I don't get to plan weddings often. Will you let us do this for you?"

The four of us looked to one another for a quick confirmation and voiced a resounding "Yes!" And that's how it happened that we set a wedding date for a week later. Short notice for guests and florists and caterers, but perfect for us. There was a great flurry of well-wishing and gratitude, and then Victor and Bella were off in their Maybach. I looked at Cole. He looked at me. We started to laugh. As did Roger and Jesse.

"Having you with Cole and me feels like a wedding gift," I said to them. We had a very silly group hug, and then we all went our separate ways to attend to our individual parts of the new life we were building. Cole had a restaurant kitchen to open in little more than two weeks. Roger had a *restaurant* to open and our first fund-raising gala to organize. Jesse had a safe space to carve from our corner of the big, scary city. I had food choices to make that could even save lives if I got it right. And as I headed back to my office, I said to myself, "I think I'm home. Yes, I know it. I'm home!"

The End

This is a first edition from
Audacity Books
Please visit us on the web at
www.audacitybooks.com
For information, please send your request to
info@audacitybooks.com.

IIT'S THEIR WAY is a contemporary gay urban romance with a little edge. It is Volume 2 of Bruce K Beck's **Tolerance Trilogy**. It follows Volume 1, **THIS IS GOD'S COUNTRY**. Look for the **Obsession Trilogy**—another collection of edgy contemporary urban gay romances—Volume 1, **INK OBSESSED,** followed by Volume 2, **OPERA OBSESSED,** and Volume 3, **LOVE OBSESSED**. Also by Bruce K Beck, his **Love Trilogy: YOU'RE SURE TO FALL IN LOVE**, **LOVE AND THE EPIDEMIC**, **AND LOVE ENDURES**, For updates, and for occasional gifts and offers, please subscribe at:

www.audacitybooks.com/#subscribe

Many thanks to Walter Maas for his generous wisdom. And to Richard Kutner for his classy edits. I turned to Tanya Lvov for advice about Russian matters. I thank her, and her husband Arkady, for their help. Tim Barber of Dissect Designs (www.dissectdesigns.com) signed on as a cover designer for my first novel, and then became a friend. You're Sure to Fall in Love, indeed. This journey would not have been possible without the example and the teaching of Joanna Penn at www.thecreativepenn.com. I am delighted, Joanna, to add this volume to your long list of books you have enabled. No doubt you will hit your one million mark any day now!

Bruce K Beck is both a writer and an accomplished chef. His novels, including the **Love Trilogy,** the **Obsession Trilogy**, and the first two volumes of his **Tolerance Trilogy**; are available online and wherever books are sold. Before turning to fiction, Beck authored ***PRODUCE: A FRUIT AND VEGETABLE LOVERS' GUIDE***, which was called "gorgeous" by ***The New York Times***, "a dazzler" by ***Bon Appetit***, and "the most spectacular food book of the year" by ***The Boston Globe***. His next book was ***THE OFFICIAL FULTON FISH MARKET COOKBOOK***, which was called "invaluable" by Jacques Pépin, and "a treasure" by Irene Sax of ***Newsday***. And Rex Reed said, ". . . you'll love this book. It's like a movie!"

www.ingramcontent.com/pod-product-compliance
Lightning Source LLC
Chambersburg PA
CBHW050407190726
48284CB00007BB/2469